I0535537

Ice

JONATHAN LOVEJOY

Copyright © 2015 by Jonathan Lovejoy

 Armageddon Publishing
All rights reserved.

Cover: *Beside the Seaside*, 1903
William Adolphe Bouguereau (1825-1905)

ISBN-10: 0692591141
ISBN-13: 978-0692591147

For every Cynthia

The waters are hid as with a stone, and the face of the deep is frozen.

Job 6:16

Snow Girl

1

Why the cold?

I ponder this benign question. This casual observance, whenever I go to my daughter's room at night. My little ghost, the icy cherub, complete with the requisite disdain for her mother, though not in malice. Our time has begun to cool to be sure, but the coldness in my heart—the shadows of my daughter's growing life are not my concern. I fret, I worry because the cold I feel every night in Miranda's room is in the air around me—blossoming from my breath in fog. Feeling like winter crystals on my fair skin.

But the living winter has passed, and it is the dead of summer's discontent. And though the fireflies have twinkled aplenty in these southern evenings, and the night breezes have no memory of winter's kiss,

I (Cynthia) stand touching the door of my daughter's room, marveling at how cold it is to my fingertips this time. More than ever, I long for another soul to tell this to, knowing I cannot even tell my own mother, because such a flight of reasonable fancy would be too perturbing for my poor mother's jittery soul.

I turn, moving timidly down the hall, undisturbed by the darkness of this wee hour, undeterred by the scant four between here and six o'clock. A middling job, a piddling boss with her glasses and power hungry eyes peering arrogantly, contumeliously at me every day. Four hours, eight hours of sleep. What does it matter, because they both leave me hunched over my office desk in kind. Dreary eyed, coveting the passing of the minutes, trying to invoke the quitting hour through sheer force of will.

I go back to bed, too nervous or too fearful to invite sleep. Eyes rest awake in the dread dark, enticing, alluring the hidden shadows to rise up. Let the closet demon scratch out its warning, if it must! Scorn to the silly fairy, the wood nymph that may alight upon the windowsill and look in with black button eyes. And what of the silhouette that may stand at the foot of my bed, stygian, peering at me with dark green eyes of serpentine? What power hath they to frighten even the blessed children?

Fear is what I understand now, as I remember that my daughter's behavior had changed suddenly, like nighttime over a winter horizon, extinguishing the light of day. Quickly, overnight, our bond had become strained, while the daughter braved her 13th year, surviving the seventh grade madness. There had been a transformation, a transmogrification, from a girl of social promise in blonde doll do, to a golden-haired maiden, instantly more beautiful, older than her years. Introverted, folding in upon

4

herself like a day flower after dark. Needing no one. Shunning the company of her best friend—a worried, sleepless mother.

If only. If only that was the ice of warning, the truth of this cold descention. And this is the night I believed that courage was gathered whole, when I was going to confront miss Miranda Auburn about her sudden reclusiveness, her new obsession with Icee drinks, and strangest of all, a near intolerance for food not much warmer than room temperature. And my daughter's eyes. Yes, those azure pools, cerulean, but now a full shade lighter as is her hair. Like a Norse princess, waiting impassively for her mother's throne.

Is my daughter's skin more pale? This, I cannot tell. Does she play in the sun, go swimming with her friends, or to the mall on these balmy afternoons? Or does she prefer the gray of rainy days, and the cool of the evening? Is this the warm, shining, radiant Miranda I once knew? It is not.

And still, after these many months (three years worth), I pray that what I had seen that winter was inconsequential. The snow had fallen like white powder the night before, cold, unmelted. The ground is an ocean of white as I drive home from the 8 hour-a-day prison. I park, stepping out into the snow, wondering why my princess is not in the yard with a flock of other girls, enjoying the first school bus killing snowfall. I brave the trip from the car, crunching up the whitened walkway, cursing briefly my lack of husband. The front door opens into plush domesticity, which is not as warm as it should have been, as though the heat had been off the entire day.

Miranda, Miranda is the call from thin, pretty lips and white teeth. A blonde Cutie-Mom, but not beautiful, comfortable in athletic curviness, secure in unremarkable prettiness. This plain-pretty leaves her black gloves and white full length coat on as she hurries to the thermostat, clicking it on, glancing out the sliding doors in delight that her blondie is playing in the backyard snow. Then, motherly frustration, tinted with guilt, when I notice her wearing only a pair of blue jeans and a short sleeved pink T-shirt in the cold. Instincts click, and I rush over to the door, stopping just before sliding it open. What I see holds me fast—something tranquil, but powerful…

Miranda is tending to a row of at least six snow figures, growing taller from left to right, from the first which looks like a miniature white blob, to the sixth or seventh, which is as tall as she. Miranda is moving her hands skillfully about like a sculptress, which would not have mattered at all, if she had actually been *touching* the figure. A crude statue, fashioned in the form of a little girl, appearing as though it had been carved from a block of thickly packed snow.

A primitive sculpture it had been, but formed well enough to remember. I will never forget the look in my daughter's eyes when she finally noticed me coming towards her from the house, or the fearful way she knocked the emerging masterpiece to the ground, clawing and kicking at the others, terrified, as if she had been caught engaged in some forbidden, unnatural act. I ask her about the big statue, bewildered by Miranda's short sleeves and stuttering fearfulness as she tries to explain how she made it. I order my pink-shirted kitten into the house, and take a long look at the fallen snow child. Kneeling down, removing my glove, touching what is not quite a face, noticing that the snow is not snow at all, and is as smooth as a porcelain surface.

I lie still now. Remembering this harmless thing (or is it?), not caring that the bathroom mirrors never fog when my daughter showers, because her water is never warm enough to create any steam. But is my daughter's pale skin still warm to the touch? It is.

I've heard them sing of sunny days

They often seem too far away

My mind drifts to a place of divine warmth, a pristine summer's day. There, I reside in hope and joy, walking with my daughter, whose hand is warm and smooth, though her eyes are as pale blue as winter ice. My daughter stares up at me with loving malevolence, shocking my soul until I understand that I am inside a dream. I claw at the veil of sleep, hoping to break through, finally opening my eyes. Unable to move, unable to breathe inside the ice tomb. A pitiful howling scream, then finally a true awakening, back into my real world of summer's dawn.

Daylight. Warm rationality. Reason rules the summer morning. Today, there will be no office. We will take a trip together. A long drive down east, to where we can walk the sandy beaches of Hatteras, and glimpse the lighthouse unafraid.

I rise from sleep. I slip into my cozy, plush bathrobe, drifting down the hall in a new confidence that the cold had been created by my silliness, my own fears projected onto my poor daughter. Inside, I feel as warm as a tropical breeze. I touch the knob of Miranda's door…

I am shocked by the iciness, the freezer cold on the gold metal. Quickly I turn the knob, opening the door, amazed as it crunches across the floor as I push, scraping a circular path. I stand still, mouth locked open, frozen deep in the new revelation before my eyes, hanging coldly down from the top of the window and every shelf in clear, sharply pointed ice crystal.

isney's snow girl. That ice boy from the comic books. I couldn't tell you a single thing about either one of them, except that they both share a profound likeness to something that my daughter can do. Something that I have suspected for quite some time, but have been afraid to let the truth inside. I've read that the truth is revealed in three parts, to protect the observer from complete annihilation. The revelation of the truth. The realization of the truth. And finally, the devastation of the truth. Which is cataclysm.

As my beautiful *sixteen* year old ice princess sits quiet on the sofa, while I stare helplessly out into the haze of this new summer morning, I can hardly gather the pieces of what is left of my mind, soul and body, which may as well be scattered about the room all around her, laid out like shards of shattered ice crystals at her feet.

A whimper and a quiet sniff rescues me from the precipice of my own destruction, drifting at me from somewhere behind me. I blink, wondering if the well of tears has coated my eyes enough to cause weeping. Surely, the tickle down my right cheek tells the tale.

"What am I gonna do, Mom? I'm a *freak."*

Wiping my eyes, I sniff the rest of my tears away, still unable to turn from the window and look at her.

"You're not a freak, honey."

"Well then what would you call it? That happened in my room when I was in my *sleep."*

Why can I not turn to her, even on the call of her second little squeak and whimper? Am I resentful, because whatever this is that has entered our lives has plunged me into the depths of fear and despair? Why don't I just run over to her and shake her, and demand that she give up this power forever? What keeps me from running over to her in full motherline rage and regalia?

Is it fear?

"When I was a little girl," I say, sniffing, wiping my eyes again, "I can remember that the house was always cold. Even in the dead of winter, my mother kept the heat down so low I nearly froze to death. I had to do my homework in my winter coat. She hated it when I would turn the heat up and try to warm the house. And in the summertime, like it is now, she ran the air conditioner until it was as cold as the snow inside. I would lay in the bed and shiver sometimes, whether it was January or June, it didn't matter. It was actually a relief to go outside in the summer. In the summertime, I could get warm outside."

"So you're saying I got this from Aunt Lucy?"

Aunt Lucy. Grandma Lucille.

If you stop her from calling me Aunt Lucy I will slap you silly, she had said. Mother's hands were cold when she grabbed my face that day. Strong, cold hands.

"Maybe. She loved ice cold drinks in the wintertime. In the summer, we spent a lot of time at the beach. She loved her white bikini. And so did everybody else. Somewhere in the world right now, there's probably over a hundred different beach pictures of my mother floating around, taken by a hundred different cameras."

"It's no wonder. She's got the biggest breasts I've ever seen."

"The biggest anybody's ever seen," I say. Laughing a little. Glad for this brief diversion. The big, flopping distraction of them.

"What about school? How can I go back to school now? What if I'm sitting in class and something happens?"

"You can control it, can't you?"

"Yes, but sometimes…sometimes I feel like I… like its gonna happen on its own."

I finally turn away from warm beach memories of cold breast queens, walking over to where my blonde, blue eyed ice princess sits in devastation and ruin.

"I could join a circus," she says. "I'm a freak anyway."

"What exactly *can* you do, honey? How does this 'ice thing' work?"

Ice

In my mind, I see the words *I don't know* form silvery in a cold mist when she opens her mouth to speak, instead standing up mysteriously, all long legs and long blonde hair, walking in contemplation over to the sliding glass door, pressing all five of her fingertips to it for a moment in deep concentration, until I notice her breath appear in a frosty mist, as she presses her hand fully to the glass. When her palm is flat against it, I am unprepared to witness the impossible happen, as the glass slowly begins to frost over from her hand outward, as if in the throes of a sudden winter's cold. This continues until the entire glass is frosted white, from her hand up and down to every corner, creaking under a stress surely unimagined for itself—as I see a layer of crystalline ice begin to form from her hand, spreading across the entire door from top to bottom. I watch this miracle occur in disbelief, standing up from the plush, ivory colored sofa, wandering over toward where the old, smooth surface is being done away with, being converted to a surface of beautiful, crystalline cold. This icy surface (like frosted office door glass) soon takes over the entire glass door, until we are both shocked by a sudden, loud *snap*, and a rain of shattered crystals falling to the floor, from the space where a sliding glass door used to be.

I go over to the remains of my sanity, picking up the heaviest piece of it that I see, amazed that it bears little resemblance to what form it lived in, and is now part of a field of shattered pieces of truth in cold, crystalline form.

Jonathan Lovejoy

Lucy's Misfortune

$\mathscr{L}$ucy's misfortune was three fold. One, her breasts were so big that she was basically unemployable. An extremely pretty, a beautiful, shapely brunette with a set of birthing hips coming off a small, curved waist. *Hips wide enough for both lanes*, her sister used to say, a problem compounded by a pair of breasts that are simply enormous, hung low and wobbly by tragic necessity, as to lift them all the way up would make her look like she was carrying two watermelons in her bra. Warehouses and factories were the only places she's been lucky enough to find steady work, since her husband left her with nothing, to marry his slim hipped, small breasted mistress. This, being the second part of her tragedy, that she was unlucky enough to be stuck in an assembly plant, folding display boxes all day like a crafstwoman, or packing whatever goes into them on an assembly line for a measly nine dollars an hour, which, with overtime, barely affords her the money for rent and utilities, let alone food for her and the other mouth to feed. Were it not for the mercy and generosity of a sister more fortunate than she, a sister married to a corporate clone and living in the suburbs, she wonders how she would have made it all these years, never seeming to have enough money to make it beyond the basics from month to month. There is always something to buy for the other mouth to feed, it seems. Which brings her to the third part of the truth.

Lucy Auburn's misfortune is three fold. The big, super sensitive breasts, that sometimes ache her with desire even in the middle of her workaday tragedy. Two, the bad luck. With bad jobs, and her condition of poverty passed through the generations. Poverty perpetuated by a stingy, selfish sister, who shares with her an end of the world secret so shocking as to be apocalyptic to behold. A secret she carries in shame, that *no* other human being would believe from here to the Second Coming. A secret that gets her money from her sister, to help her address the third part of the tragedy which is her life.

As she drives home near the midnight hour, from the second shift in Hell on Earth, Lucille Auburn's tragedy is threefold. Her breasts. Her poverty.

Her daughter.

Jonathan Lovejoy

Lucy Auburn

Rides the Wind

Lucy Auburn rides the wind. On the eve of eschatology.

Breasty poverty mother. Fair skinned, brunette beauty. Small waist and all hips—a wide ride coming and going. Breasts too big and heavy to fathom. Weighing her down with perversion. To drown her beneath the surface of desire. Choking her in the ocean of regret.

Lucy Auburn rides the wind. Gliding into the working class neighborhood of nothing. Tiny, one story houses of disillusionment, so many with the nerve to be painted white. The color of hope. Falsely, and unfreely given.

Ice

Lucy pulls into the driveway of lost hope. Gazing at the house of broken dreams. Wishing she could just get back on the road and keep driving. A wish wasted into the space of her life. Laughable, ridiculous even, having not even the gas in the car to make it anywhere else in the world but back to work the rest of the week.

Lucy steps out of the car, into the starry approach of midnight. Dreading the arrival of this day. This hour. Of what pain that has built up over the years. Of what pain must be released onto her daughter.

Lucille Auburn rides the wind. On the eve of eschatology.

Gliding through the icy cold, late December night. Somewhere beyond the advent, between the Nativity and the New Year. She goes into the tiny, white box that dares inhabit space in the shape of a house. Feeling the heat blasting from the vents. The heat of disobedience. The heat of opportunity.

Lucy Auburn clicks the heat to the off position. Craving the touch of winter in her body again. A mistress of the cold.

Lucy goes to her disobedient daughter's bedroom down the hall. Opening the door to Cynthia's room. To my room.

I am twelve, when the spirit comes to me. I am twelve, when the spirit of Lucy Auburn hath come.

You're not asleep, she says. *You're just scared, because you forgot to turn the heat off before I came home. I'm coming back into the room in a minute. To punish you.*

Lucy Auburn goes to her tiny excuse of a bedroom. Feeling the spirits of divine luck. The spirits that torment her with desire. Those that burn her insides with blue and black fire.

She disrobes quickly, and without ceremony. Naked in front of her mirror, gazing at the bane of her existence. At the first part of her tragic life hanging free. The pendulous, bulbous things hanging like giant bells to her waist. Where the sound of them tolls for thee, Mother.

In resignation and defeat, she removes the member from her bedroom dresser drawer. The realistic member strapped on. A full eight inches of death, slid up and around her hips. The instrument of her daughter's destruction. The fire in which she will burn.

Lucy Auburn rides the wind. On the eve of eschatology.

Strolling helplessly in the nude. Soft padded footsteps creaking the old house wood. Strolling through the house air, air far too warmed for her taste. Feeling what punishment she must give her daughter. Knowing which punishment must surely be given.

Lucy opens the door to her daughter's bedroom. Listening to the creak of the old hinges. Having no pity.

Sit up, she says. This, the girl does. Shocked to grief by the sight of her mother naked. Gigantic breasts hanging low and exposed. The realistic member strapped on below.

I am twelve, when the spirit came to me. I am twelve, when the spirit of Mother Auburn hath come.

She walks in epic confidence into the room. Telling me to get up, and to take off my nightgown and underwear. This, I do. Standing exposed in front of her. Hips already bulbous with promise. Breasts undeveloped and ripe for the taking.

In an expression burdened by a frown. Lucy Auburn touches her lips to her daughter's breasts. Unphased by the twitch that rocks her daughter's body. Unmoved. Unmerciful. Grabbing hold of the girl's bottom with both hands. Pulling the nipple deep into her mouth. Devouring the whole breast in a single, epic sucking. Letting her tongue caress the nipple again during the sucking pull. Relishing her daughter's body in twitching again. Releasing the nipple in a hard, popping sound.

I was gonna turn the heat off, Momma. I fell asleep and I forgot. I was so cold.

I told you to leave it off, she says. *You disobeyed me.*

I won't turn it on anymore without asking. I promise.

The mother lowers her own eyes in defeat. Nearly having pity for the girl's hopeless begging. Nearly.

Get on the bed. Lie on your stomach, she says. This, I do. Feeling the heavy presence of Predestiny climb on the bed on top of me. Feeling the brush of burning desire against my back. Making her body shake once in grief. A single, mighty twitch of defeat.

Lucy Auburn spreads open her daughter's bottom. Letting the spit fall to her rectum. Placing the head of this pain to the door of Chastity. The door of this perversion passed down.

Lucy Auburn pushes through the veil. Listening to the tiny house echo with a scream. A scream that degenerates into a weeping.

Lucy Auburn pushes on. Sliding every inch of this pain into her daughter's bottom. Sliding her hands down underneath her daughter. Placing her hands between her daughter's legs. Her body on fire from her daughter's weeping. Her daughter's sorrow.

Lucy lays still upon her daughter. Squeezing her hips. Pressing them down. Unable to fathom the level of pleasure. The level of pain, from her fingers at the door of innocence. To her member strapped and pushed in. To the center of the heat in her body. The heavy breasts laid bare on her daughter's naked back.

The woman is unable to resist her hips in squeezing. Marvelling at the involuntary pressing. The squeezing that happens on its own. Feeling the member inside her daughter as an extension of her. As part of her life grown and blossomed.

The fire in her breasts ignites in full. Spreading to the flames come to life in her groin. Touching at the center of her body. Rising a groan from her voice burdened by trembling. A long and deep, shaking moan that lingers, until every drop of breath is out of her lungs.

The feeling in her body pulls air back into her lungs. To prepare her for what must be.

The feeling explodes into every corner of her body. Causing her to screech an unholy shriek into their tiny space. Into the condemned space of their lives. Holding her body captive. Refusing her a deep breath. Threatening to pass her out from the trauma.

In the aftermath of Predestiny. In the throes of agony come and gone. The woman lies still. Nude, on top of her naked daughter. Barely able to perceive this waking reality. Barely able to remember her name.

Lucy Auburn rides the wind. On the eve of eschatology.

Grand Canyon

Mother

rand Canyon National Park is the classic cure for what ails us. A gift delivered to me by way of a bizarre browsing through my satellite TV guide, three long nights ago, when I was treated to what has got to be the most violently bizarre fight between women that God ever allowed into a mainstream movie. I didn't know what to expect when the title called me to press the button, to Encore Westerns, no doubt, where I saw two actresses named Ann Miller and Penny Singleton display the heart of Amazonia in blonde and brunette beauty. A good girl in goldilocks and frills clawing and slapping and pulling and wrestling a black haired bad girl in tight jeans to the floor. Whatever the characters were fighting about may not matter at all, as much as the two actresses themselves in this old, black and white Western, who seemed commissioned to put the dark heart of woman on endtime display, two performers obviously infused with the spirit of genuine combat, who were going at each other in what was a real, knock down drag out fight like they meant to hurt each other. It was a bigger thrill than I have ever gotten from any glimpse at some skinny naked girl licking and lapping with some ridiculous man on one of the late night softcore secrets, which have often yawned me into changing the channel from pure boredom. This fully clothed black and white Western girl fight squirmed me more down there than I've felt in a long time, to tell you the truth, especially when the hitting became so hard and real, and the bad girl's top was ripped open. I even left it there for the rest of the movie, remembering nothing of it, beyond the behind closed doors fight these two women had, which burned the message from the title *Go West, Young Lady* into my heart and mind forever.

And so I spoke this self same message to my grieving daughter three nights ago, telling her that she only *thinks* the Grand Canyon is lame because she's never been there. But after the truth turned our glass sliding door into something that actually started to *melt* in the sunlight, I knew it was time for us to take a breather in this August heat, before the reality of her eleventh grade year reached up and grabbed us under the September Autumn Moon.

We were smart enough to book a helicopter ride over this once in a lifetime trip, to hopefully get something of a thrill for our time, to hopefully have our minds briefly taken away from the grim truths of our reality. As if I didn't have enough of a burden to carry already—first it was Lucy's breasts (which she sometimes smothered me with while my mouth was gagged with a cloth and her stocking tied around my head), and now, it is my anointing as the mother of the world's first real life ice witch, ice queen, or even ice goddess notwithstanding.

The fear of this is lifted briefly on our ride, as we lift up into the air over the canyon near sunset, when the sun first begins to change itself to amber, to foreshadow its journey toward the western rim. And at the moment when I believe this mile high wonder is as beautiful and spectacular as it can get, our helicopter ride flows us smoothly around a corner of plain desert terrain rising to the sky in front of us, to reveal the glory of God in creation, in breath taking little rock mountains that stretch into the distance, rising above the tiny Colorado river below— high walls of layered rock carved a mile deep, jagged rock walls striped with the earth's history, centuries of upheaval and stress, eons of turmoil and trouble written in stone, in layers of red and brown striped beauty along the high canyon walls which grow more breathtaking as we approach them nearby, the helicopter gliding us down over the river, and between the walls where the handwriting of time and history are naturally displayed. Briefly, I am reminded that there is some beauty left in the world, some places untouched by the corrupt hands of God's two legged creation, where the message of his glory is free to shine, without hindrance from the manmade lights of earthly progression.

We are lucky enough to be the only two on this ride, being here at the end of August instead of the beginning, when every other parent and child in the world seems to have left fantasy behind, to deal with the approaching reality of Labor Day, and the dark promise of another school year to suffer through.

After our glorious flight through the canyon, where the walls are layered in red and earthen mystery, we disembark our heavenly trip onto the Western Rim, where the so-called skywalk awaits. With a few others who intrude on our space, we walk onto the horseshoe shaped walkway, rising 4000 feet over the canyon floor below, where the raging Colorado River bears resemblance to a glorified trickling stream. And what I've heard is true that yes, pictures cannot do this place justice, and stepping out onto this glass platform will slow your stride down to a shuffle against your will. Knowing that this thing is sturdy enough to hold 800 people, withstand 100 mile per hour winds and a magnitude eight earthquake does not take away the feeling of being suspended, precariously, in mid air—at a height greater than every skyscraper in the world.

I wonder how many people this thing can hold, when my mind feeds me an involuntary image of my blonde doll in her faded jeans and bluebird blue tee, dropping to her knees in quiet rage, and end of the world frustration, slamming both palms of her hands into the thick glass underneath us, sending waves of a cold through it that it could not possibly be prepared for, changing the glass into something related to *ice,* until it becomes brittle as a saltine cracker under their feet. I wonder how many lost souls this glass U-thing could hold, how many souls it would see break through the brittle ice-glass, and plunge 4000 feet screaming to their eternal reward. How many of them would hit the bottom of the canyon unredeemed, and spend a thousand years in outer darkness before they were judged and thrown into the lake of fire and brimstone.

I cannot ignore the brunette mother's unabashed audacity I see, one of the dozen or so tourists left straggling out here at the end of the summer. I am unable to stop my staring, at this forty something year old sexy-pretty, comfortable in her brunette jenny-braids hung down well past her shoulders like a raven haired Pippi Longstocking, unashamed to have one of her corrupt hands deep in her daughter's back pocket, while the daughter—who looks like full blown seventeen, at least, stares down into the canyon as nonchalantly as she can, trying not to be weirded out by her mom's clue in public, that the secrets behind closed doors are monumental, and what I know of it runs wide and deep at the twilight of humanity.

Whether or not she is a lost soul is immaterial, I think. Only that her soul is capable of bringing such a dark power into the world, and plunging her seventeen year old, bubble hipped beauty into a depravity that cannot be mentioned. What of the myriad perversions do they share? Which delicacy hath she partaken of in the upper room? Is it to hold her daughter close to her in the nude, and burn a red bruise onto her little big hips with the palm of her hand? Is it to take one of her own mature floppies into her hand, and rub the nipple like a cavewoman trying to start a fire with a stick and a rock—rubbing it up against her seventeen year old daughter's puffy nipples until her own body doubles over, when the tension breaks into her body? Or does she have the beautiful girl do the bunny hop on top of her nude, praying the girl's pitiful young libido will strike lightning to her tight, bubble hipped young body and cause her to scream? How many of these hopping sessions has the mother, this mother that I see—how many of these bouncy sessions has the mother laid on her back in awe and amazement, their hands locked together, how many times has this Grand Canyon mother been unable to keep her promise to herself, and not began to shake and grunt before her time? How many times has this hopping daughter watched in satisfaction, as her pathetic, flop breasted mother was lost in the pain of an orgasm she could not endure? How many times has this Grand Canyon daughter watched in satisfaction, while cultured civility broke like shattered crystal in her mother's tormented expression? Knowing that she won this battle again?

I watch Bunny Hop and her daughter's secret on display, as the orange sun falls below the Western Rim, and the world turns toward the evening day. I walk to the edge of this oblivion beside my own blonde teenage beauty, receiving the glance from the jenny-braided mother, a smile laced with a shocking level of understanding, and a glance that lingers into a brief stare. *I have my own blonde doll to do*, are the words that threaten to appear in my brain from the motherline curse, and I am more than glad to place a kiss hard and firm upon my daughter's fair skinned cheek, which I am amazed brings only a casual smile from her so far beyond her years, and a reaching of her hand across my body to mine. Without looking at me once, she stares out over the Canyon depths, in the world after sunset, her right hand reached back, past the front of my hips to my right hand, our fingers locked together in a message—that makes me close my eyes, and takes my breath away.

$\mathcal{O}$lympian breast beauty hath skipped a generation, and landed firm upon my daughter's body. What mine lack in sheer size, they make up for in flip and flop. They are in the key of G minor, a depressed and melancholy key, that has them sag at great length when I bend over. And if I were to jump with any effort at all, they would flap and clap against my body with enthusiasm. And though the gigantomastia that my mother had threatens my daughter's chest more than mine, my mother's breast sensitivity is surely passed down to me, which I have noticed many times over the years in a weak moment in front of the mirror, but have struggled to ignore. Only a few minutes ago in the bathroom, in the hotel of this magnificent and desperate last trip of ours to sanity, I could not resist a nude and hippy stance in front of the mirror, where I took one of the long G minors up with both hands, and pulled the nipple deep into my mouth. For the first time in the forty six years of my miserable life, I gave in to this, having never done it alone and away from my mother, shocked that it may have been the most profoundly pleasurable thing I have ever felt.

The shock of it torments me even now, while I sit on the edge of the hotel bed, listening to my daughter in the shower. Knowing that I am just one of the many who are tormented by this curse. The Curse of the Motheress, who haunts me at this moment in unseen spirit form. It is the spirit of Amazonia, a secret devastation that is a pandemic at the end of the age, the last taboo in the wilderness of humanity, here at the twilight of human history.

Which witch is the bitch who switched on this end of the world libido? Is it really the Grand Canyon mother I met in the lobby of this very hotel, who spoke to me about something that my mind could only process in bits and pieces—that such things actually exist in 3D space, that there are really socially well adjusted, sophisticated, middle class women who engage in such things?

"I'm going to ask you something," she said. *"It's pretty deep, so... please don't get offended. And I'm only asking you this because I've done it myself..."*

The beautiful, brunette woman leans in close to me, and says...

"Have you ever been with your daughter?"

And as I sit here still listening in fear to my daughter's shower, I'm even amazed at my own ridiculous inability to be real with this woman, bewildered at my own phony, hyper-hypocritical...

"What do you mean 'been with' exactly? Been alone together on a trip?"

And this beautiful woman slides closer to me in the lobby of this hotel, clearly embarrassed at her own inability to push easily past the barrier of cultured civility and say…

"Have you ever fucked your daughter?"

And throughout time and history, what questions ring the chimes in a soul, to send ripples though the timeline, across the space time continuum itself? The only answer I am even strong enough to form through the humiliation, the fear, and the shortness of breath is…

"Wow, that's…wow. That's an interesting question. I… I wish I had time to see where this is going, but my daughter and I have to get some rest before our trip tomorrow…we have to drive all the way to Virginia, so… it's been nice meeting you…"

"Alison. I'm a real estate lawyer from Oklahoma City."

And this 'Alison Browne' hands me the most beautiful beige business card with her name in big, brown letters with 'and Associates' printed over 'Real Estate Law.' I take this card with my hand trembling noticeably, which causes her to smile big and wide, then suppressing it with a big, pink tongue to her big, pink lips, tucking them in the most perfect, brunette, sensual beauty.

"Whenever you want to finish this conversation, be sure you call me…"

"Cynthia."

"Cynthia," she says, holding my hand tight, staring me down from my neck to my knees. *"Of course."*

"It's been nice meeting you…"

And though I try hard to pull my hand away without wrenching it in total rudeness, I am unable to escape this lustful strength she displays in her grip, this failed, bitter former prosecuting attorney—compensating with her hugely successful private practice—pulling me close as we stand up, whispering in my ear...

"My daughter Laura said that your hips were beautiful..."

In the heart of memory, I see this sensual lawyer whispering in my ear as if outside my own body, the sound of the people in the hotel lobby suddenly transforming into the sound I continue to listen to with dread, finally hearing the sound I have been in fear of this entire ten minutes, which is the sound of her barely warm shower being cut off completely.

I don't know what I am more afraid of at this moment. The end-of-the-world spirit that has gripped my groin, or the end of the world truth that even after a ten minute shower, there is nary a particle of steam, I'll bet. Barely a droplet of condensed water vapor anywhere in that bathroom.

Which is the witch that flipped the switch in my body, I wonder? Is it Alison Browne, the attorney at law, the professional mother lover in disguise? Or is it Lucy Auburn? That giant breasted, brunette beauty that was my mother, who subdued her looks in short hair and no makeup, content to look dumpy in her loose shirts which failed to hide her assets completely, which made her look many pounds heavier than she actually was? The low wage assembly plant worker that was my mother, held back and held down in life by bad luck spirits from dawn to dusk, until she had to give up her quest for success? Is it Lucy Auburn that tickles my fancy at this moment, that enhances every sound my daughter makes in the bathroom, as if I have super hearing, even to where I think I can hear the ruffle of the towel against her bare bottom in repose?

Is it the sight of my mother straddled atop me when I was a freshman in high school, one of her giant breasts pulled deeply into her mouth that has grabbed me by the throat from behind and yelled into my ear that *it's going to happen, bitch, whether you like it or not!* Which witch has flipped the switch in my body tonight, O Lord, that has placed the forbidden fruit in my hand, and made it impossible for me not to pull the sweet taste of it into my lips, and swallow it as bitter wormwood to my soul?

A spark of revelation flashes through my spirit when my daughter steps naked out of the bathroom, her face covered, rubbing her hair wildly in the towel, partially hiding two globes pitched all the way up in G major, and as bulbous and round as two cantaloupes hung in 3D space. A G cup is the low estimate to what I see, which are two big, white breasts pitched up past G into a phantom key of H, to create the most distinctive figure for many miles around in any direction, and surely the biggest of any girl her age in her school. I find myself having to look away, unable to *not* be embarrassed, and a little shocked by this bold, new behavior.

"My God. When did you suddenly become a nudist?"

"Since now,' she says. "Staring at me. Smiling a little, wiping the water from her ears and her wet hair. "Are they big enough for you?"

And as if called upon, by the spirits that well dictate who we are, and who it is we will become, she holds her arms out to the side, and bobbles the two Gee Whizzes in space like two wobbling water pillows attached to her body. In my mind's eye, for a brief second or two, I see her grandmother Lucy, when she did it in front of me when I was twelve. Like a game.

"Okay, you can stop now," I say. Pretending not to watch her put her big towel on mercifully, smiling to herself as she walks over to the bed and sits down beside me. I keep gazing at the wide screen hotel TV, unable to turn and look this newfound bravery in the eye.

"I'm sorry I embarrassed you," she says. "I've always wanted to do that. They're so *big*. I couldn't help it."

"That's fine honey. It's just you and me."

"Why can't you look me in the eye, then?"

In full, motherline authority, I turn in false faced confidence. Staring her directly in her eyes. Eyes as blue as the skies over arctic summer.

"Your eyes. They're not as pale as before."

"It comes and goes," she says. "Sometimes they're so pale they scare me."

"*Tell* me about it," I say, shaking my head back and forth a little, in profound confirmation of what apocalyptic shock her stare can provide.

"Thank you," she says.

"For what?"

"For this trip. For not freaking out because I'm a monster."

"Oh honey," I say, pulling her in close, kissing her firmly, lovingly on her forehead near her wet hair. Then, as if compelled by a spirit, again in the middle of her forehead.

What motivations do gather themselves, in the hearts of womankind in secret! What spirits have touched both my daughter and me, to send us careening forward in depravity! I am unable to remove this second kiss from my daughter's forehead, without releasing it in classic, loud kissing sound. Staring this beautiful girl directly in her eyes now.

In a boldness bestowed unto me by blood, and by the spirits of the woman who gave me life, then took it so abundantly. Whether or not Miranda can hear my heart beating, this I cannot tell. For it is loud enough in my own ears to drown out the sound of my own breathing.

And in the wake of this muffled rhythm in my ears, I lean forward to the face of innocence and beauty, to touch corruption to these lips of chastity, feeling my ears ring a melody above the rhythm of my heartbeat, down to the center of my chest and beyond. The feeling draws in a heavy breath of its own accord through my nose, in a kiss pressed tight and uncompromising to my daughter's lips, until I am finally able to pull myself away from her just enough to breathe the words…

"Oh God, what have I done. I'm so sorry."

"It's alright Mom. Look at me."

This, I do. My eyes already hazed over with a lifetime of regret.

"You think I didn't know how you felt?" she says.

"But honey we're not supposed to do this."

"Why do you think I came out of the bathroom naked?"

"What do you mean?"

And this answer she gives, pushing past the barrier of her mother's personal space, laying a sucking kiss to my neck that rolls my eyes up, and twitches a pissing twinge to my groin. *Breast goddess,* are the first depraved words that flow to my perverted spirit, followed by, *put your daughter's tits in your mouth…*

This, an order bestowed to my soul with authority, causing me to fumble her towel away and lift one of her gigantic breasts to my mouth, pulling the nipple in as though they could nourish my body for Christ's sake, my brow wrinkled and cheeks sunken in from the sucking pull, feeling my *entire body* respond with a sudden and rapid tension, a tension that grows with each and every suck, until I feel as though I may go mad from the sensation, forcing me to lay her down backwards, still fully clothed in my lavender collar shirt and faded jeans, my head bobbing up and down on her breasts in slow, determined rhythm as if my very life depended on it, unable to release her nipple even if I tried.

Oh my God, are the whining words that drift from my daughter's mouth, as we are locked in this rhythm and position—every deep, fleshy pull of her breast fully up into my mouth, being guided by a lust in my body stronger than any I have ever thought possible, rising me up to a plateau higher than any I have felt naked or fully clothed, holding me clamped to her big breast as though my survival were in tow, until I hear her whining grow less controlled, drifting the words *oh my God, Mom* out in crescendo, repeating her last syllable in an explosion of girl sound into the room, a shriek unabashed and unrestrained, ending in a high pitched siren in the secret, hidden air around me.

I continue this profound sucking through her trembling and shaking, through the rise and fall of her voice, holding her down in the Virgin's Intercourse without mercy, to fully immerse and anoint her with her hidden and unseen life's calling as a *breast goddess,* passed down from the queen mother who bore me, and sent her spirit through the timeline to my daughter and me.

But what plateau my body has achieved must surely be relieved, lest my soul not be soothed from the fires, upon which it hath come bereaved...

You need to cum in your tits, are the third whisperings of words that flush in me from head to foot. Causing me to pull her up slowly, though she be spent from her own devastation, standing up and disrobing every stitch of cloth from my depraved, condemned body—until I am at last bent over to slide the small, white underwear cloth down from my widened hips, feeling my own breasts hung low in wobbly G minor, which my daughter is so smoothly compelled according to her gift, to grab a hold of by the nipples while I bend over, which twitches my leg once very hard, causing me to stand still in fear that all of the tension in my body is about to break.

She needs to spank your ass, is the fourth whisper of depravity that lights up my spirit, making me stand us both upright in front of the mirror with her beside me. A grim, determined look on her young face, as though she is angry at me for having taken her innocence, for bestowing upon her this motherline curse—the Curse of the Motheress, the craving for this unspeakable behind closed doors grief and tragedy.

As per my command, she raises her white hand far back, to bring not the fires of ice and cold to my backside, but the burning of blue and black fire, quivering the fat of my buttocks without compromise—many, many times ad nauseum to burn, until I must cry out from the dual agony in my body, that of a pleasure morphed into pain from inside, and pain morphed into pleasure from my skin on the outside.

She needs to slam your tits together so you can cum, is the fifth whisper of depravity in my spirit, as she stands tightly against me from behind, holding my long, flopping breasts with each hand, smacking them together in 4/4 time, in solid, steady rhythm of the ages, that rhythm of not too fast and not too slow, where the frustrated desire for faster cannot be appeased, to rise the plateau in the body back up to the impossible, holding me there, begging me not to touch myself down below past my abdomen pressed, to allow the spirit of Amazonia to caress my body as it will, to burn my soul in the fires of endtime devastation and ruin.

And upon my daughter's expert and obedient direction, I close my rolling eyes to the deep knowledge and authority on her expression, to feel an explosion of feeling begin in my breasts, to ignite a fire in my womb beyond my groin, where these in turn do meet at the center of my body, to double me over in shrieks and screaming, and the apocalyptic shaking of my entire body in rolling thunder and cataclysm.

Alison Browne

Rides the Wind

 lison Browne rides the wind. On the eve of eschatology

Real estate lawyer extraordinaire. Mother of one. A closeted lesbian, buried deep in the suburban myth and method. A purveyor of the pornographic fantasy come to life, manifested in reality. Feelings and desires from childhood suppressed. Repressed so deep that the pressure erupted like a new geyser upon her daughter. Three years ago, when Laura Brown was fourteen. So appropriately on Halloween night, when this spirit came to call. After seeing the little superhero girls on Halloween. When she saw the innocent pre high school spirit at rough play, when the Batgirl doll had her daughter encircled in a rope. Her little Catwoman doll. Young curves so prodigious and new. Young breasts and thighs pinched and pressed so deeply by the rope prison. A sight having flashed a bolt of lightning from Alison's brain—from her brain, to her heart. To her groin.

Alison Browne rides the wind. From the chill of an eighth grade Halloween night, three long years ago. Across a three year landscape of perversion. The cold, howling winds of predestiny. Having held it in check, kept it locked down as a private fantasy. Loving her husband. Servicing his successful, suburban need. Channeling the truth into a legal career. Riding the wave of bad luck from the prosecutor's chair, into the good luck of a private practice office chair. Having found her calling. As a brunette never blossomed into bottle-blonded beauty. Desires buried deep. Put there when she was a girl of twelve. Put there by her mother's best friend. Done on babysitting night. Her mother's small waisted, big hipped, flop breasted friend. A suburban wife, she was. Mother of three teenage boys.

Alison Browne rides the wind. On the eve of eschatology.

In the heart of her fervent memory. *When I was your age*, her mother's best friend says. Small waisted. Heavy hipped. Italian tint about the eyes, nose and mouth. *When I was your age, my Momma shared something with me.*

The woman takes twelve year old Alison by the hand. Pulling her up the early evening stairs to her best friend's bedroom. With her best friend's daughter.

Quick work is made of every stitch of cloth. The woman whose features bear the hint of the Funicello mystique bends down, fleshy and naked with her best friend's daughter. The two of them standing nude by the bedroom mirror. Having found at last, a place to plant this motheress seed. Tongue in full ice cream like repose. Circling her head wildly, with her tongue wet and pressed hard against the girl's nipples. The nipples of her best friend's daughter.

Alison Browne rides the wind. On the eve of eschatology.

The Italian mother stands up naked and beautiful. Waist small and fleshy besides. Hips heavy and quivery. Breasts hung long and bulbous when bent over.

She raises her licking to the girl's neck, grabbing her by the head. Ice cream licking her from her neck to her lips. Slurping the years of repression unleashed. Pulling both the girls lips into her mouth. Pulling her tongue besides. Grunting the agony of its awakening. The spark igniting the flame in her hips jiggled by a twitch. Turning the girl around to face the music. The music of her reflection. A melody played in a somber, suburban key.

The woman presses the front of herself to Alison's bottom. Pressing the knob of her desire into the young girl. Pinning her arms to her sides. Her features burdened by pain. The frustration of tension unreleased. The fury of energy not yet unleashed.

This is what my momma did, she says breathlessly. Eyes closed in recollection. Sounds filling the summer evening dark around them. The daytime dark of the evening day. The sound of uncontrolled breathing, flesh slapping hard against flesh. Holding the girl's arms so tight against her. Shifting one hand up to the girl's throat. A grip tight enough to cause a small choking. A labored breathing heard by the woman.

Holy Mother of GOD, she says gruffly. Staring anguished at the young girl's face. A face red with trauma. Trauma of the mind. Of the body. Of the soul. A spirit being rattled to pieces. A psychology being shaken to the core.

The woman's features take the character of fear. The agonizing wait for pain impending.

The woman calls the name of God and Holy Jesus. The Lord and Savior of her Catholic faith. Reaching out to them for mercy.

The woman's sanity flashes away. In eyes rolled back to blindness. Seeing only the angels and statues and candles of her darkened youth.

The young girl feels the trembling. The mighty quivering of flesh pressed tight against her. Amidst the sound of a woman lost in the throes of bellowing. The sounds of sanity come and gone.

Alison Browne rides the wind. On the eve of eschatology.

$\mathcal{O}$n the night of All Hallows Eve. Three years before her daughter was seventeen.

Hair still its original, exotic brunette, swirled and pinned up with more style than is normally possible. Face powdered and painted with maximum skill, to put beauty on full, end of the world display. Full length, sparkling white evening gown. Low cut cleavage in the firm, rounded key of C major. Diamond tiara tucked firmly in place, to complete the image of her heart uncovered. Devastating beauty, labeled for the little preteen beauty queens and Disney princesses to ohh and ahh at in their hears, the weight of disillusionment and even despair threatening their pretty little Halloween features, when a real beauty queen opens the door and bends over at them with her huge bowl of fun size chocolate candy, the gold fleck in the "Miss Universe" sash burning out their mother's eyes in witchery. The sorcery of beauty on their little stage, runner up for Miss Oklahoma, fifteen years seasoned and matured. Hips curved out from the motherline, breasts bloated toward the D minor key. *Whoa,* the typically funny, overweight mom among them says. *Honey, my self esteem is low enough as it is,* the other moms in full cackling laughter not touched by fungalooga, but genuine in its attempt to hide their misery. Smiles, laughter, obligatory questions asked and answered.

Miss Oklahoma USA, first runner up, she says. *I came THIS close to the big one.*

You mean Miss USA? one of them says. *You almost got into THAT pageant? The Donald Trump Miss USA on TV?*

This close, she says again. *But you know what? That blonde bitch who beat me lost in the first round…*

And the laughter continues. Lingering. Loitering on the lawn. Every Mom and daughter finally waving goodbye to the real life beauty queen. Drifting into the night.

On All Hallows Eve. Three years before her daughter was seventeen. Alison Browne closes the door of her two story, brick suburban palace. Unable to manufacture a smile behind closed doors. Sickened by the sight of the candy. The grotesque mixture of every fun sized chocolate drug she could find. Baby Ruths and Butterfingers galore. Mounds and Almond Joy, Snickers and Milky Way in store. Three Musketeers and

Nestle Crunch. Twix and Kit Kat she had grabbed, then finally Hershey Bars and no more.

Alison Browne gazes a divine reflection. Dreading the impending sound. The sound of metal against metal, slamming at her nerves, reverberating through the house.

How come they never use the doorbell?

There is often so much to fear, from a fateful knocking at the door.

Another hour come and gone. Until every witch and ghoul, every ju-on ghost and Disney princess has gone their way. The beauty queen hears the chimes drift nine times, to remind her that she is at the precipice. The edge of oblivion.

Alison locks the rest of the candy treasures away in the kitchen. Determined to tell any others that there is no more. To lie to them. To watch their crushed little faces turn in disappointment. Knowing only in her heart that all she can care about for the rest of this evil night arrives at the ten oclock hour.

On the eve of mankind's final departure. These stars do drift the passing of another moment along the timeline, until her fourteen year old kitten is dropped off at the door. Full blown, adult Catwoman gear stretched tight across her little body. A young body so tight with promise. Hips bubbled out already in mocking. To torment those who might dare to endeavor a look, on how such youth can display such mature, unearthly beauty.

Seventeen is the lie her face and body tells to every stranger. Hiding the truth of who she is. The virgin truth.

Alison waves goodbye to silver SUV luxury in the dark. To the mother and the other daughters taken away. Taking Laura's hand. Taking her daughter's hand, escorting her into the Halloween House.

The tallish, shapely brunette beauty queen, still in diamond tiara and evening gown. Miss Universe sash still in place. Cleavage still pitched between C major and D minor. Escorting her daughter through the softly lit luxury, past the lamps and comfort cushioned sofa—past the silly paper ghosts on the staircase rails, past the giant, beautiful broom-witch silhouette on the wall pointing upward. Upward towards the frigid, dreary space. Towards the nighttime upper room.

Why are you mad, Mom? I didn't do anything, did I?

I'm not mad honey, she says. Sniffing away a tear. Kissing the back of her daughter's hand. Escorting the two of them into her palatial bathroom. Closing the door behind them.

Mom what's wrong? Why are you crying?

The voluptuous beauty queen can only touch the lovely chin of her beautiful little Catwoman. Raising her pretty face up for the look. The stare into her eyes.

And then, the weight of a lifetime of regret takes the mother by the shoulders, lowering her down to her daughter, crown and sash firmly in place. Kissing the masked young beauty gently on the mouth. Lifting the kiss. Lowering it again in fullness. In the power of womanhood.

On the night of All Hallows Eve. Three years before her daughter was seventeen. She lifts the black cat mask up and away from her daughter's beautiful face. Turning her to the mirror. The space around them is suddenly alive with the daughter's confusion, voiced by the sound of the zipper being undone, from the back of the girl's neck, all the way down to the small of her back.

In the mirror, the girl sees the catsuit slide off her thin, white shoulders, exposing her little lace bra underneath. In the mirror, she sees the beautiful woman look down with determination, unlatching the little bra, sliding it down and away from the underdeveloped little breasts in firm, perky B minor solemnity—watching the exotic woman lower her head to the puffy areolas, twitching a mighty twitch when the woman in the mirror gives suck, pulling nearly the entire breast deep into her mouth in anguished desperation, releasing it in one loud, popping sound, repeating this to the young girl's astonishment, moving her head to the other breast to do likewise in a greater, sucking pull. As to the epic feeling in her groin, the girl does not know. She only knows to return her mother's kiss with enthusiasm, using it as a limb to grab onto in this raging flood of feeling, holding onto her mother's tongue for dear life with her kiss.

She watches the woman's beauty lift up and away from her. Burdened by the heavy weight of Predestiny, and the unendurable pain of what is meant to be. To relieve this suffering inside, she fumbles with the full length of her long, sparkling white gown, sash still in full gold flecked splendor, raising the dress high enough to reach between her legs, inside her underwear cloth, to slide out the long, thin member chosen for this inevitability, strapped on and tucked into her underwear in the hour before her daughter's arrival.

The daughter sees the mother's lovely expression in the mirror, hardened with anguish and solemn commitment, feeling the mother's fingers at her backside, stuttering, struggling to open the door of the forbidden.

The woman's finger pushes into her rectum. Making her tense up greatly. Staring into the mother's hopeless expression, a look burdened by a driving force, by the awakening of a flame ignited the color of blue and black.

The girl whimpers her disbelief, her disapproval, when the head of this member touches, impossibly, the outside of her rectum. To warn her that the door of chastity is not easily crossed, and the barrier of innocence falls in pain and trauma. And in keeping with this dark promise, she watches the mother, she *feels* the mother push hard up into her, to send the breath from her lungs across her vocal chords with fervor, evoking a loud and violent shriek into the bathroom walls around them. She opens her eyes again, to see the beauty queen grab onto her body so tight, watching her, feeling her thrust again, evoking a second and lesser shriek and such a pitiful *ow, it hurts* as to be heartbreaking to the spirits of compassion, which can have no power in the presence of sadism unleashed.

The sound of her daughter's pain causes her to take her hand down from her daughter's throat, grabbing onto both her daughter's young breasts, closing her heart to the sight of blood down below, slamming herself in repetition into her daughter in full, having no pity for the girl's shocked, teary eyed expression, knowing only that her pounding must continue, until the feeling in her breasts is married to the feeling that rises in her groin.

And she slams into her daughter with much force and violence, until she understands what tragedy hath befallen, when the feeling in her own breasts is ignited in full, causing her to open her mouth in shock, to wait for the impending trauma at the base of her member strapped on.

And she holds on to her daughter's breasts as the energies meet at the center of her body, to explode a cataclysm in every part of her flesh, to cause her daughter to witness her mother's face twisted in an angry grimace of agony, and her beautiful mouth opened in a scream passed down through the ages from east of Eden.

Grand Canyon Night

My daughter's breasts are as sweet milk to the palate. Having awakened me in hunger and grieving through the night in our hotel of dreams, in the midst of a paradise of rolling thunder outside. It is a sudden nightstorm, born from the early evening clouds that had begun to gather in the evening day, after the glory of the canyon was revealed in its end-of-the-world splendor and majesty. And I remember that these clouds had suddenly appeared as if from nowhere, beginning to blot out the stars one by one, until eventually, even the star that rules the evening was hidden behind the evening cloud veil. And in keeping with the spirits of my depravity impending, these clouds have gathered somewhere in the midst of this Grand Canyon night, to release a powerful energy from themselves, as if on the heels of pent up rage and fury.

The music of this storm has awakened and accompanied my hunger twice already, the first time being just after the stroke of midnight, where I fumbled at my daughter's nightshirt like a sick drug addict in the darkened room, putting my mouth to her nipple hard enough to cause her intense pain—the painful whimpering, the quiet little 'ow's' she made reaching into my body and causing it to roll over on top of her completely on its own, from being only partially on top of her, to being fully over the top, with my groin pressed tightly against hers, finding that I was unable to release her breast from this single, sucking pull.

In the brief heart of this memory, I am raised up on my arms over top of her, with her breast pulled up into my mouth, slamming my groin into hers in that special rhythm between fast and slow, until I can hear the deep, animal grunt and groaning pouring in muffled sound from my nose, my mouth having been clamped down on her gigantic white breast for no less than two or three minutes while I pound her without ceasing, until my body's energy pushes out the gruff sound, which reminds me of a howling heifer prophesying in a grassy meadow.

From this drowning I emerge, head spinning, barely able to see straight in the dark softly lit by the glow from the bathroom, light left on with the door slightly ajar. I had held on to her nipple in total commitment, breathing and grunting though my nose until the wave had completely passed, finally releasing her nipple in a hard, sucking pull. Laying selfishly on top of her in the midst of this storm of grieving, taking deep breaths through my open mouth now, feeling the rhythm of our heartbeats in tandem and misery.

The second awakening sees me in the midst of this powerful storm again, no more than an hour later to be sure, having laid on top of her again selfishly, but this time working on *both* of these giant, remarkably firm globes together and one at a time, until my lust eventually moves my hand down to her warm, wet groin, rubbing my hand feverishly and without mercy across her swollen *clit*oris, until she sends a teenage girl siren though the walls of this hotel.

My daughter doesn't get off as much as she *shoots* off, so that anybody wandering by our door at this late hour would know that as surely as it's raining 'til the morning, somebody just came in that room. And the third hour of this awakening is where I am now, having slid my own breasts across hers, down her stomach and across her waiting groin, compelled in the storm, on her leg, to rest my lower self and take up my breast in one hand, and put the erect nipple against her erect clit and rub it like I'm trying to start a fire.

And I notice that while her reaction is simple arousal, mine is the rapid buildup of another lightning strike in my body, centered in my breast at the nipple, a sensation that causes me to keep rubbing fast, staring down at it in rapt amazement and attention, watching her pink little groin swell up again, pressing my hips just once against her leg while it is happening, noticing that the longer I rub my nipple against her clitoris, the stronger the buildup of sacred energy in my entire body, until I can feel this full tension take over, evoking a whimper from me that foreshadows a growing fearfulness, of what on earth it is that is about to happen to my body.

But I press on through this apprehension, stubbornly rubbing my nipple against her where it's at, until I suddenly feel my groin clamp itself to her leg, struck by the lightning shot from my breast down to the center of my body, causing my entire body to shudder as the tension breaks, sending a series of heavy, strong gruntings from somewhere deep inside me and out through my voice, as I feel the waves of energy torment me from my breasts to my buttocks, to my groin and back to my breasts once again.

Mommy's Little Girl

11

We've spent the rest of the summer in deep depravity and delusion. Deep perversion, which is the spirit of the modern mother daughter dynamic unbridled. Trading breast orgasms ad nauseam, with one another as if we were two unrelated lesbian lovers—me, being a full grown, fully mature woman a full 46 years along, licking and lapping my birth daughter like an ice cream cone without reservation and without remorse, deciding to bury the guilt in entitlement and personal privilege. Truthfully, I consider myself lucky to have had the pleasure of this forbidden fruit, and this little breasty slice of heaven—end-of-the-world gifted besides. Why should I feel guilty for doing something that so many are doing in secret behind closed doors, and will never mention it to another living soul?

But I had the privilege just a month ago to have met someone who basically asked me *"Have you fucked your daughter,"* while confessing to me that she had fucked her own. The pornographic myth of the mother daughter exchange club and the mother lover's society are nothing of the kind; they are every bit as real as a church club or honor society, with more church club and honor society participants than can possibly be believed. I know this by firsthand knowledge, being a perpetrator of it myself, though I am so called 'socially well adjusted and normal.'

And there are so many mothers that I can see in my mind's eye, who have not crossed the line literally, but have worn a path down to the dust walking back and forth across a *figurative* line, where walking up behind their little blonde beauty queens at the sink rinsing dinner dishes for the dishwasher, and wrapping their arms around them and planting a sucking kiss on their neck is nothing to them, then whispering in the big 17 year old's ear, *"you still mommy's little girl?"* Getting the confirmation look from the daughter that yes mommy, we are mind-fucking each other from here to eternity, the cushion of your breasts against my back clits and tits me to oblivion.

I have watched this very scene play out before me in the park, when the young mother is preoccupied with her stroller, married or no, and the older mother has her arms wrapped around her grown daughter like a twist tie, barely able to hide the fact that if they were in private, she would drop her pants and bang against the back of her daughter's jeans until she shook. And for us, besides this depravity we embrace, is the delusion we hold on to, believing that this first day of her eleventh grade year is somehow a good idea.

"This isn't gonna work, Mom. You know it and I know it."

"With that attitude, of course it won't. You need to stay socialized, Miranda. You're spending enough time alone as it is."

"I've got enough to keep me busy forever, you know. Don't act like you don't get it, Mom."

She turns to look out the passenger side window, and I half expect to see her blow an icy breath at the window half covering it in fog.

She doesn't.

"This thing you can do. It might not even be permanent anyway. What if it goes away in two years or something. You'll be eighteen years old with no high school diploma, hiding in your mother's house."

"Maybe that's all I'm meant to do."

I notice the drifting of her voice as we approach the school in silver SUV semi luxury, rolling to the front of the busy 1st day campus. This beautiful, fair skinned blonde girl, this teenage blonde woman looks out the window at the teachers and students walking and talking all over the place, as if the mere thought of attracting even the smallest amount of attention from them would be unendurable. And though I try not to notice it, I have to admit to myself that yes, the cold I suddenly feel in this car is *not* the figurative kind.

I ponder this benign question. The thought that continues to haunt me in my dreams, and into the waking hours of my life, such as it is.

Why the cold?

The spirit of regret follows me all the way home from Miranda's school as I drive, causing me to have to drift onward as through a veil of fog off a summer lake, on an ice cold day in Autumn. The chill of what I've done is in the air, as if I have driven a white Bengal she-tiger to the door of that school, opened her cage and left. But as I pull into the comfort of my suburban driveway, I shake my head, smiling a little at the silly thoughts that have plagued me since she got out of the car, picturing the entire school buried in my daughter's gift on full display. God only knows the depth and power of such an otherworldly gift, of what terrible, apocalyptic purpose I fear it may have under the sun.

While I prepare to spend the day in epic gratitude that I don't have to go sit in that office cubicle all day, my heart is burdened by the delicate, fragile creature I left behind. Picturing her adrift in loneliness and uncertainty down the busy halls, able to survive this jungle wilderness of raw, youth emotion by way of pure prettiness, which allows her to escape the uncompromising flashes of cruelty gathered and thrown. Even her own friends from the tenth grade, from the end of her last school year look at her strangely at first, some even with a touch of apprehension, noticing that she grew several inches taller, that her blonde hair has lightened even further, and the blue of her eyes is more pale than they remember. These are the nice, somewhat nerdy girls she was comfortable with last year, all of them having grown into the echoes of their plain, future selves, while their friend Miranda seems to have blossomed into something the cheerleader squad will soon be drawn to like a butterfly to a wild, white rose in a grassy field.

It is Fate's compensation and protection, I suppose. Nature's way of keeping her away from human antagonism, which could prove deadly for the unlucky person causing her pain. As the cold, September sun drifts high into the sky, with me riding around town from one store to the next, looking for the clear crystal figurines to add to my collection, stuffing my face with a dry, overpriced hamburger from some restaurant I should have avoided—none of this can take my mind from my ice princess, imagining her at the big, open cafeteria entrance in the lunch hour, feeling as though she has hit an invisible wall, knowing that to step down into the busy sea of empty chatter has become an impossibility.

I can see her in my mind's eye, turning in defeat away from the hoarde of cliques and clichés, buried in false hope and delusion about their future, drifting back down the hall, past the lockers that seem to stretch into infinity, finally coming to the big, double doors of the school library. She notices the glasses and the pinned up hair on the middle aged, mountain breasted Mom of a librarian, wondering why she is wasting her time trying *not* to be beautiful. My daughter obeys the motheress spirit inside, and goes over to the sensual Ms. Ramone, asking the lady bent over with butt and bosom, *"where are your books on witchcraft?"*

And my daughter allows herself to study the woman's peaks and valleys, climbing up and down every mountainside in the brief span it takes for the woman to tap and click her computer screen until she finds out—writing down the section number on the back of an index card and handing it to her. Having hardly any idea why, she decides to engage the archaic curiosity, the nearly obsolete task of browsing a shelf for an actual library book to read.

Past the empty tables and lonely shelves, she glides toward where the non answers to her strange, end of the world condition lie in wait. *Mom never said that Aunt Lucy was a witch*, she thinks, rounding the corner to where Ms. Ramone said the witchcraft books were.

Miranda nearly jumps an inch off the floor from the spark that flashes through her body, completely startled by the long haired, long skirted girl with big, scared eyes. Lurking alone.

" *A*re you a witch, too?"

The question reaches inside Miranda, causing her to open her mouth to try and respond. The question looms like an intersection, where the choices are spread out in three, which road to travel.

"I'm just kidding," the girl says. "I'm not a witch." Although I do *dress* like one and I *look* like one, and they've been accusing me of *being* one for two years. I'm Emily, by the way."

"Nice to meet you. I've seen you before a few times. I'm Miranda."

"I know," she says. Tucking her lips, glancing inevitably from the gold spun hair and winter eyes, to the magnificent bosoms displayed in the sky blue collar button down. "You're one of them."

"Who?"

"If you'll pardon the expression," she says, "The in crowd."

"Me?"

Emily Watson looks away from the books that say *The Power of Witches* and *Witchcraft and Sorcery* for one more good look at the endtime expression of Barbie Doll beauty from head to toe.

"I swear I'm not," Miranda says. Feeling the accusation unspoken. "If I was, would I be in the library?"

"I've seen them in here sometimes," Emily says. "When they're forced to have to do a bibliography for a research paper. So, I guess this is your year right?"

"For what?"

"Your coronation," she says, adding the book *The Salem Witches* to her armload of interest pending. "This is the year when Miranda Auburn finally becomes a cheerleader. Finally gets the football player boyfriend. Finally becomes homecoming queen for the first time. Then queen of the Junior prom."

Emily's somewhat dismissive, judgmental brushing past her is enough to cause what fires there are waiting inside her to ignite. To flicker.

"You sound like you're accusing me of something," she says, following Emily to the nearest table. Though the big, suburban Virginia school is filled with students, the library is a vast, open space of quiet disillusionment, with echoes of unfulfilled promises and despair.

"I don't know if its *accusing* somebody of something if it's true."

"And what if it was true? What would be wrong with it?"

"Well, just look at Samantha Daley. She's been head cheerleader for 2 years already. Her boyfriend's graduating this year. She drives a fucking *Tundra* to school. And she is the biggest bitch this side of the Blue Ridge Mountains. And when it comes to looks...you've got her beat hands down, honey. If they get a hold of you, their gonna turn you into one of them. A self absorbed, conceited Barbie Doll, who gets off on making other people's lives miserable."

Miranda is suddenly swept away by the girl's insight, glimpsing off into her own perceptions, and the truth of how the girls act, the ones at the top of the food chain.

Emily glances at the remains of her attack, seeing a beautiful, blonde girl's face awash with a sudden and powerful humility. Lips tucked in, eyes glazed over in a somber distant stare.

"I'm sorry," Emily says. "I'm really sorry. You don't deserve that. Its just those damned ice queens. People think those movies like *Mean Girls* and *The Fab Five* are fiction. But that shit is real, Miranda. Just this morning they walked past me, and one of them said *Witch Hazel,* then Samantha and the rest of them started screaming with laughter. I swear to God, I thought I was gonna die."

"I'm so sorry," Miranda says. "I swear to God I would never do that to somebody."

"I know. I can tell. It was bad last year, Miranda. But I have a feeling…I have a feeling I'm in real trouble this year."

Unbeknownst to her new friend, Miranda perceives the flash of fear, betrayed by her somber, melancholy expression.

"Lets get out of here," Miranda says.

"Where?"

"Lets go outside."

The two of them rise on the current of a new grieving, drifting towards the future as one. As partners in whatever current of happiness or pain there is that awaits them. With her books in hand, they leave the busty, hippy Ms. Ramone to her valley of broken dreams, leaving the library behind and drifting down the hall.

In their approaching vision, the white paper taped to one of the lockers haunts and mocks them as they get closer, forcing them to accept the reality that yes, this white sheet of paper is taped to Emily's locker, and yes, the word *witch* is branded upon it in lipstick the color of tears and blood.

Jonathan Lovejoy

Emily Watson Rides the Wind

*E*mily Watson rides the wind. On the eve of eschatology.

Riding home on the bus in the spirit of hope. In the naiveté of expectation. Believing there is a future to be had.

Emily disembarks her rolling yellow chariot. Braving the flash flood of laughter that ensues when she stumbles and nearly falls getting off the bus. Walking onward, ivory white face flushed in humiliation.

Emily Watson walks the road well traveled. Down the working class streets—the poorest neighborhood on the route. Tiny houses lost in a struggle. A struggle to appear relevant. Sad, tired efforts in lawn and garden décor.

Ice

Emily Watson rides the wind. A figure dressed in a tight, pullover black shirt. Draped over the long, flowing skirt in faded black cloth. Black boots halfway up to her knees underneath. In league with hair long past the length of her shoulders. Hair as black as the feathers of a raven in winter.

Emily Watson rides the wind. Turning from the path well traveled. A prisoner now of the one less traveled upon. This, the beaten path to the domestic. The path to bitterness. The road to discord and family chaos grown.

Emily steps foot into the quiet of disillusionment. Into the echo of secrets hidden in the walls. Hearing among these fearful spirits, the sound of her mother's voice, *"Is that you? Get your ass in that kitchen and wait for me!"*

This, she does. Rolling her eyes in contempt. In exhaustion laced with fear.

Emily Watson steps into the kitchen. Seeing now the source of her mother's rage. The pile of dirty dishes left in the sink from the night before. Remembering Kate Watson's voice in the theater of her mind. A set of dishes that were supposed to be done before school this morning.

"You see those damn dishes?" the mother says. Floating in witchiness from the back bedroom down the brief hallway. *"How much more of this lazy, disobedient bullshit am I gonna have to take?"*

"I'm sorry I forgot. First day of school and everything."

"Bitch are you getting smart with me?"

"No. I really did forget. I'm sorry."

The next moment rings a chime. The music of a thunderous slap across the face, from the tallish brunette in Amazonian strength and beauty. Curves on full, gray skirted display. High heels in place, in preparation to play the Mall Game. To walk the floor of Macy's for the next six hours, in underpaid glamour and false glory on exhibition.

The beautiful woman takes her daughter by the ear. Twisting it without mercy.

"I forGOT!" The daughter screams in pain. Face twisted in sorrow and agony.

Emily Watson rides the wind. On the eve of eschatology.

Upon her mother's orders, she leaves the dirty kitchen to itself. Going to her mother's small, back bedroom. Her mother in step directly behind her. An angry brunette at over five foot ten in her heels and gray skirt. A skirt stretched across hips spread to infinity.

In the bedroom, the daughter is made to strip every stitch of cloth. Down to the bare skin.

The mother grabs her daughter's breasts. Twisting them at the nipples. Twisting them to cause agony. To hear the screams of pain. Telling her *"you might as well save the tears bitch, cause you're gonna need 'em."*

The mother goes to the closet. Where the black caning rod lies in wait. Making her daughter put her hands behind her back.

In full, corporate blouse cloth of white. Skirt in shades of corporate gray. She lays the cane in repetition across her daughter's breasts. Across the front of them. Face in full makeup. Eyes grim with determination. Ruby lips turned downward in anger. Hand in full, rapid caning motion. The black rod of correction raised far back. Brought down from a full distance away. Listening to her daughter's screams grow hoarse. Hearing her voice go gruff with strain.

Ice

Upon her mother's order, the seventeen year old turns around. Turns to face the mirror. Unable to fathom the creature she sees. Unable to fathom the suffering.

Upon hips widened as her mother's. Upon a hip spread extraordinary in her youth. The cane lays down another chorus of red striped pain and suffering. Done in the same spot over and over. Until under duress, the new scream comes out on its own. Forcing its way out in a new tone. A deep, woman's scream.

Emily Watson rides the wind. On the current of heat slicing through. On the current of pain and grieving. Made to turn around when the one hundredth stripe is laid. Looking at her massive bottom in the mirror. At the truth laid in the ironic colors of independence. Bruised and striped as the colors of Americana. Burned and bloodied into her skin. From her buttocks to the back of her thighs.

Her mother stands in front of her. Close in front of her. Telling her, *"this is your year, bitch. The year when you learn whose in charge. Now...put your lips to mine."*

This, she does. Enduring a hard squeeze upon her bruised, bloody bottom. Having to moan upon her mother's lips. A moan in begging. In weeping.

Emily Watson rides the wind. On the eve of eschatology.

Jonathan Lovejoy

Cry of the Motheress

orrow drifts up from behind me in spirit form, draping itself around me like a white faced, black haired *ju-on,* reminding me of how I have ruined my daughter's life in the Grand Canyon Suite. The skies above us have responded accordingly as we drive home, drenching the earth in a cold mist of Autumn rain.

"I met somebody today," she says.

"Who?"

"This kind of weird, goth girl named Emily. I met her in the library at lunchtime."

"The library, huh?"

"I just couldn't go in that cafeteria. I wasn't in the mood."

"What about all your old friends, you know, Ashley, Jennifer, Chelsea. Did you see them?"

"Actually no, I didn't. Not once all day. I think it was because we don't have any of the same classes. Plus, I only talked to Emily. It seemed like a thousand people were everywhere between classes. I'll probably see them tomorrow."

"Are you going out for the squad this year?"

"The *squad?* "

"Cheerleader of course."

"God, why does everybody want me to be a freakin' cheerleader so bad. I don't want to be a cheerleader. A.k.a. *bitch*leader."

"A *what?* "

Miranda turns to the rainsoaked glass, smiling a little to herself. Tracing an unknown message in the brief echo of fog on the glass.

"It's just something Emily said."

"This… *Emily*…you said she was 'goth?' Just how goth is she?"

"She's not a *witch,* Mom. At least, I don't think she is."

"Well, if you say she's goth, then I assume she's dressed in black from head to toe."

"So what if she is?"

"With the requisite dark sleep circles," I say, motioning my finger in circular at my own eye. "Black fingernail polish. Long black skirt. Weird, black vest thing over a black t shirt. Big, clunky black boots."

Without a word, this blonde, teenage doll pulls every word from the air, comparing them to the image of her friend in her memory.

No match.

"To tell you the truth," she says, staring into her memory, "there's a Greek-Italian thing in there somewhere. She might be the prettiest girl in the whole school."

"I doubt that," I say. Taking this opportunity to remind her of who we are. Touching her on the knee. Rubbing it once with sensual abandon. Sliding my hand far over the edge of it, then back up and across the bottom of her thigh. This, done with nary a glance in her direction, but having to open my mouth to breathe a quiet, sudden breath inward, when she folds her hand around mine, and squeezes it without pretense. Without remorse.

"So, you think you'll make it then? Back in school, I mean. As if you really belonged there?"

"I'm gonna try. It interesting, because halfway through the day I thought I wasn't gonna make it."

"Until you met Emily."

Still holding my hand, Miranda looks at me with such a depth of understanding, such a profound and committed stare of absolute clarity that I become vulnerable for a brief fraction of a second in time, as if a part of me beyond my control acknowledged the power she possesses.

From her Grand Canyon awakening. Through the remaining heat of August, and into these cold, misty September days, we have traded *orgasms,* my daughter and me. Using each other's bodies for our own perverted pleasure, to take out a generation's worth of suffering on each other, passed down from Lucy to my beautiful daughter and me. There is no ex-husband, no future boyfriend that can approach the brightness of this light we have found, as it is the hidden, forbidden glory behind Creation itself, where knowledge pulled from the forbidden tree has its desired effect, to carry the two of us away in fantasy come to life, where daughters hold their mothers down naked in bed, with their mother's breast pulled up into their mouths until the mother must grunt and shudder from the tension that breaks in her body. Where mothers lie full in top of their daughters backs, their hands buried underneath their naked daughters between their legs, while they slowly, tragically slam their big hips into their daughter's bottom, until one of them must give in to the trauma that rises, which is a guaranteed spasm of the mother's jiggly, wiggly big bottom on the front end or either the back end of her daughter's fervent scream.

In the renewed, and dedicated knowledge of who we are, we disembark our rolling, suburban chariot into this endtime mist of cold rain, with me waiting patiently under my umbrella, waiting for her to walk undeterred through the icy droplets at her leisure. Taking my hand, joining me slowly underneath the beige umbrella, which is the color between hope and despair.

I am a perverted bitch are the words that reach into me and hammer my soul to a ringing chime, as I am at the edge of the bed on all fours, long breasts hung down in udder audacity, big bottom facing my daughter who stands at the corner of the bed, leaned over my back in grieving, waiting for her inner voice to speak, having already rubbed every inch of my body into a throbbing tension, her strapped member hung down big and ready, with my head hung in the throes of something akin to shame. And as though hearing the echoes of my guilt whispered, she delivers my punishment in the hardest spank I have felt in a generation of years, when my mother was burdened with the grief of my life and time. My body lurches forward in the wake of the loud whack against my flesh, shocking me into a new revelation, that of this, she is called as completely as I.

And in quick succession to the first, another whack to my big bottom lurches me forward again, but this time sending a wave through every jiggle of my flesh, so that I know that surely, I briefly felt the swing and pull of my own breasts hung down from my body. And a third, and profoundly hard hit confirms my suspicions, that too many more of these will have the most ironic affect on my body, and will cause every inch of my flesh to quiver like an icy chill in winter.

But at the promise of this rape and special deviance, she reneges, and instead puts the head of herself strapped on at the center of me from behind, but only to prepare it for another truth, one that I had not considered for the two of us yet, but as is true with predestiny, all things have their place along the timeline. And this member she wears is full size, already not for the faint of heart, which she touches to my other place in brief warning, causing my breath to go unsteady at once, as if it could stop the punishment that she has chosen for me.

And without further hesitation, without further ado, I feel my rectum split by a roll of thunder slowly unleashed, slid in without ceasing, until I have to lower my head again in one loud, long cry of a warrior's rage, pain endured in anger and suffering. In the wake of this, I draw a noisy breath, then groan a loud, gruff sound of pure triumph, at having endured the agony of what she has pushed inside of me.

And she begins to deliver the rest of this punishment, starting with three hammering whacks to my backside—three, thundering spanks in a single, painful spot, which cause me to groan in relief rather than pain.

And she begins to slide her lady cock strapped on, sliding it deep inside and out, inside and out, until every inch times eight is hidden deep up inside me. Then, to my back she returns again, laid down in full on me from behind, unable to hold back her vulgar victory spoken—*"do you like your daughter's cock up your ass?"* And I refuse to answer, until she grabs tighter hold of me and lurches forward, causing me to groan a gruff call again, yelling the word *yes* in all out, angry defeat.

She rests there, barely pushing herself against me, breathing, moving her hips in this anal raping, as though every inch of this member were nerve ended and networked to her body. I can surely tell, that not many thrusts hence, is the full flowering of this girl's erotic genius, this sensual gift, which is the profound ability to grow her libido to the length and width of the lady cock she wears.

She begins to caress the suffering I feel, by way of her hand across the low hanging front of my swinging breasts, which soothes the heat in my body to a warmth which begins to spread, until the fire in my rectum is put out and replaced by a cooling pressure, which radiates a pleasure unknown until it is the growth of icy hot, causing me to thank divinity in my soul for the feeling of my daughter's cock, and of what hidden pleasure this is that I have been allowed to discern.

"Rubbing your tits is gonna make me cum," she says. As I feel the squeeze and rub she gives them become more determined, more automatic, and more impossible for her to stop. And with her other hand, she delivers no further mercy or compromise, reaching underneath me between my legs, to place her hand still and firm at my proper place, my improper place, telling me *"your clit is so big,"* still rubbing my breasts without ceasing, until I feel her body begin the Armageddon Quake,

pushing out in her young voice a new depth, the quivering, woman's moan of suffering unleashed, as the wave of energy pours through her shaking body into mine.

And upon this revelation, my own devastation ensues, and I hear from somewhere in my spirit erupted, the sound of a full grown woman wailing the cry of the motheress, as the waves quiver every inch of my body and soul in weeping.

Jonathan Lovejoy

Lucy Auburn

Rides the Wind

Lucy Auburn rides the wind. On the eve of eschatology.

A prisoner of her sister's lust. A lust born when the girls were sixteen and thirteen. When Lana noticed that Lucy's breasts were developed beyond the dreams of Eve. When her training bras were filled to bursting and then some. When the thirteen year old had to be fitted for a B cup. A C cup. And then a D cup overnight. A thirteen year old girl. With the curves of a full grown woman in tow.

Lucy Auburn rides the wind. On the eve of eschatology.

Cornered in the bathroom by her sixteen year old sister. Told, *shut up and let me see 'em.* Forced to take off her bra to avoid a beating. To avoid being put in the headlock by her older sister's domination. By her older sister's whim. A sister already a prisoner of their mother's lust. A sister whose chastity was taken when she was twelve.

Lana Auburn can resist no longer. The need born from she knows not where. When she caught a glimpse of her younger sister in her underwear. In the new bra twice as big as her own. A feeling sparked between her legs like a lightning bolt. A message whispered to her ear.

In the bathroom, Lucy is forced to take her t-shirt off at the mirror. Then, she has to take off her bra.

In Lana's hands, her sister's breasts feel like two flesh pillows. Irresistible to squeeze. Irresistible to wobble.

Lana Auburn lowers her sixteen year old lips to her sister's nipples. Pulling one of them into her mouth by instinct. Unable to release the sucking that rings a chime in her ears. Holding on hard to one breast. Nursing the other for dear life.

In her jeans, Lana's leg twitches hard. Enough to shudder her entire body. A feeling that hazes her vision. Causing her to grunt deeply. Having to release her sister's nipple so she can think. So she can breathe.

Lucy Auburn rides the wind. On the eve of eschatology.

Of an instinct born by its own volition. Lana Auburn takes her own shirt off. Exposing her firm, tight B cups to the spirits in the room. Telling her younger sister to take one of her D cups in her hand, and rub it against her B minors. Tit to tit. Nipple to nipple.

This, the girl does. Rubbing her nipple to her sister's whim. To a lust born apocalyptic.

Lana stares. Watching her younger sister hold the big breast in her hand. Rubbing the nipple against hers in youthful naiveté. Lips tucked in confusion. An expression burdened by shame.

Keep rubbing, Lana says. Noticing the buildup of the same feeling. The feeling that twitched her leg only a moment ago. Threatening to happen again.

Lana's breath begins to betray her. Staring hard at the breast action down below. Feeling her lower body suddenly give way to instability. Both legs shaking this time. Causing her to stumble. To double over when the lightning strikes. Fighting the urge to scream with another heavy grunt. Holding her younger sister for dear life. Hugging her tight. Breathing hard in the wake of trauma. By another instinct born. By the whispering of the mind of Eve passed down.

Lana turns her sister to the mirror and gets behind her. Unbuttoning her sister's jeans. Sliding her hand to the warmth down below. Sliding her hand to the warmth inside. Causing the young confusion to grow. Twisting her beautiful face in the agony of discovery.

Lana rubs her sister's chastity without ceasing. Taking one of her sister's big, puffy nipples in her fingers. Tweaking. Pinching. Pulling.

In the mirror, Lana Auburn watches the heavy breasted young girl. Watching her give in to feelings beyond her comprehension. Watching her obey spirits she does not understand.

The young girl pushes back hard against her older sister. Lost in the tragedy of new discovery. Enduring the series of lightning strikes. Unable to hold in the high pitched scream.

Lucy Auburn rides the wind. On the eve of eschatology.

Samantha

" *God.* You act like I fucking *killed* somebody."

These are the words that haunt the space of my memory. For some odd reason, I can hear Samantha Daley's voice as clearly as if I was there myself, when my daughter witnessed the beginning of the end of the world.

"I would appreciate it if you could watch your language in here, Miss Daley."

The beautiful, blonde and busty Samantha Daley cannot close her mouth in principal Greer's office, turning to gaze at my daughter, and the girl the whole school has taken to calling Witch Hazel in whispers and laughter. When the words *Emily Watson's real name is Elfaba* showed up on one of the chalkboards, even the teacher who erased it had to tuck both her lips to keep from laughing.

"This is fucking *hilarious.*"

"You curse one more time in my office Miss Daley and we'll go for five days instead of three."

"What is a suspension going to do to my *f*...to my grades and my overall *record?*"

"One three day suspension isn't gonna ruin your life Miss Daley. But—"

"My name is *Samantha.*"

The shapely, middle aged, yellow-skinned beauty opens her own mouth in disbelief. The same look that a view of audacity always puts into the naïve's expression.

"...but it will teach you, *Samantha,* that you can't go around willfully disrespecting other students and making their school lives more difficult than it already is."

"You act like I cornered her in the shower and threw tampons at 'er when she got her period or something. What did I do wrong?"

"The security cameras have already *told* us what you did wrong, Miss Daley. And under the school code of conduct what you did warrants a three day suspension. I already talked to your mother over the phone and she agrees."

"She *what?*"

"Starting tomorrow, going into Monday and Tuesday, you will not be allowed to set foot on school property. Nor will you be allowed to communicate with *any* of your teachers. I would suggest you get with friends about your assignments so you won't fall behind.

"I've got two quizzes tomorrow."

The healthy hipped, yellow-brown fox takes a deep breath. Breathing in the air of modern youth, disrespect and disobedience in the room.

"Not anymore, Miss Daley."

The bubble breasted, bottle blonded beauty stands up straight and tall. Secure over the safety net of what privilege a family's money can buy.

"If you think this is over," she says, staring boldly at the middle aged principal, "you're in for the shock of your life."

"I know your father is rich lawyer, Miss Daley. He has no power over me or this school."

"You're gonna find out what power is, Haddie May."

"You will address me as Ms. Greer."

"Oh, well how 'bout Foxy *Brown?* You look just like her and you've got the same name."

"You're dismissed, Miss Daley."

"And you're *deluded,* Ms. Greer. Because if you want to know the truth? You fucked with the wrong Indian this time."

"Make that *five* days."

What invisible forces have conspired, to hold the beautiful blonde's mouth closed at this moment? That holds the words, *its coming, bitch...wait for it,* at the tip of her tongue?

With one more glance at the two tattling traitors nearby, she turns on the current of humiliation, and glides out of Ms. Greer's office, closing the door just hard enough to qualify it as a genuine slam.

"Miss Watson, I'm so sorry you've had to deal with this. These girls think they're gonna take over this school. I can assure you, that's *not* going to happen. So, you girls go on about the rest of your day and don't worry about her anymore. She'll be gone a whole week."

Ice

Ms. Haddie May Greer allows another reassuring smile to the two misfits, escorting them out of the office in as much comfort as there is left for a high school principal to give.

Miranda and Emily leave the office in nervous tension. In apprehension over what they have done. Whether or not they have raised a barrier strong enough to stop this train. This, the runaway mischief and cruelty Samantha and her friends are prepared to start, and what pathetic little lives around the school are set to be made miserable.

They walk from the principal's office, past the main desk in hope of renewal, both girls smiling to the matronly soul in charge, catching the wave of exhaustion that flows from her phone and computer station, stepping through the entranceway where there is no door to slam. Both of them relieved that there is no one standing there to greet them, to threaten them, or otherwise make them wish they had never been born. Content to miss whatever class this is—whatever drowning prison of academic nonsense that was blocked in for this hour—they decide to take this free hold in their favorite hiding place, glad for the privilege of catching another glimpse at the most voluptuous librarian in Virginia. Being in this quiet, this tranquility draws a sigh of relief from the both of them, as they stroll over to the table farthest from the door, hidden from whatever prying eyes there be that stare.

The two girls take their lonely place at the isolated table in the back corner, the choice spot for any wandering soul with the proper understanding, both feeling the call of predestiny, and the imprisonment along this mutual path unchosen.

"I feel like such a freaking *rat,*" Emily says. "You said we did the right thing."

"She had to be taught a lesson. Otherwise..."

These words are choked, by a sudden flash of revelation in her goth friend's eyes. Eyes drawn to a looking away, to somewhere in a place beyond corporeal reality. As if seeing shapes drift ghostly into 3D space nearby. Miranda turns to look, and is acquainted with what is written, concerning the nature of fear.

"Otherwise *what*, Miranda?"

These four beautiful spirits, adrift into their isolated space. The four of them stepping in power, prestige, and prettiness bordering on the extreme.

The types of fear are many. And uniquely distinguished.

Samantha Daley. Kelly LeMonde. Rosalyn Reynolds. Jennifer "Jenny Lynn" Johnson.

The four of them.

On either side of the two girls seated, they take their place. With Rosalyn and Jennifer standing nearby the raven haired witch. With the extraordinary LeMonde, and her mistress Samantha by the blonde one.

"The thing that scares me a little," Samantha says, "is that I don't think you realize how much trouble you're in."

Miranda finds herself unable to stop the requisite glance. The fearful glimpse over at her friend across the table, gazing up into the eyes of the tough, beautiful Rosalyn, who is staring Emily down like something on women's fight night pay per view. The look on Jenny Lynn Johnson's face is a bewildered mixture of contempt and pity.

"You had it made, Miranda. This was your year. We were going to make you one of *us*. You were definitely going to be a cheerleader. You could have had everything. Even money."

"You *blew* it, bitch," is the soft spoken tragedy breathed in Miranda's ear from behind her, Kelly's voice nearly making her jump from the spark of terror passing through.

"I always thought you were different," Samantha says. "We thought you were like us. But it turns out, that you're just another pretty, pathetic, *pussy.*"

The word causes Rosalyn to laugh in suppressed, giddy delight. Still gazing directly at Emily in a direct, determined dare for her to move or speak.

"You two bitches... are *dead.*"

Even while Emily can hardly resist a visible tremble, Miranda's expression relaxes to the calm of uneasy acceptance. Staring at Samantha without blinking.

"Oh... there's fight in those pretty blue eyes," Samantha says. Leaning closer. "That's the way I *like* it."

In a rage suppressed and genuine, Samantha Daley stands up straight from her leaning pose, not bothering to gaze at another soul except Miranda. Turning slowly, to drift back from this corporeal reality, followed by three others of like beauty and sensuality. Stepping in unison of spirit, the four of them, with one last look of confused pity from the ghost of Jenny Lynn, as they turn away from the lonely girls' sight, drifting back into parts unknown.

Miranda remembers to take a cold breath. Turning to see her friend with both hands over her face in the tragedy of revelation. In the drowning from the third part of the truth come ashore.

Which is cataclysm.

Samantha Daley Rides the Wind

Samantha Daley rides the wind. On the eve of eschatology.

Having left school early on his Thursday afternoon. Having hurried her three minions around in the Tundra. An end of the world truck in charcoal gray. Named for the frozen wastelands of arctic winter. Rolling Kelly, Rosalyn and Jenny Lynn to their mini mansions in the twilight. Rolling the streets of this town in the evening day. Refusing to allow the beauty of the thumbnail crescent moon to affect her. Blocking out the glow of amber across the horizon at the western gate.

Samantha Daley rides the wind. Arriving at the immense brick mansion property in Brandmere West Estates. Disembarking her rolling chariot in the evening. Back pack heavy laden with nearly every schoolbook. Prepared to spend the whole of next week in home schooling. Wishing she could be there. To lead the way. To rule from the highest social class in the school. To jump and flip at cheerleader practice. To prance and smile by teeth so white. Bottom bubbled outward in beauty known throughout. Breasts burdened and bounced in the D Major key. In grieving already to jump for them. To spread her legs open wide for them.

Samantha goes into the brick mansion home. Unable to absorb the spirits of privilege. Million dollar security. Bought by what is meant to be. Paid for by Predestiny.

Each step is powered by a promise. A buildup of energy begging to be released. The culmination of years of echoes and warnings, about to come to fruition. Where the mother daughter dynamic of their lives must join the latter day flow. Where it's transformation leads to a purpose unrestrained.

Samantha Daley rides the wind. On the eve of eschatology.

Finding her mother in her room where she always is. A privileged place of employment. A cushy, fluffy job online. Editing shopping reports. Minimum wage insignificance, to say that she has a job, at least. So that all four of her $300,000 savings accounts can be justified in her mind. So that her bygone husband's alimony and child support can masquerade as a non factor. That her friends might believe she contributes at all to her financial life.

Samantha enters Pricilla's room without a knock. Gazing at the bottom heavy, fat breasted woman in a rage unspoken. Waiting for the suburban haired, earthen blonde alimony queen to open her mouth in explanation.

Pricilla Daley looks away from her computer towards her daughter. Trying not to accept the reality. The truth of the emotion passing through her heart to the pit of her stomach. An emotion that runs her blood cold in revelation.

Without a word, the blonde steps rapidly toward her mother at her bedroom computer.

"Look," the mother says, *"there's no need of you getting angry with—"*

Her finishing thought is cut off by a powerful slap. A slap that rings true. A slap that rings a chime into her brain.

In the next moment, the woman feels her daughter's hand gripped tight in her short, dark blonded head of hair. Pulling her up in near masculine strength. Dragging her stumbling to her feet and across the room. Feeling herself thrown down to her bed. Feeling the strong cheerleader and local Judo champion slam herself down on top of her, nearly knocking the wind out of her.

Samantha covers her mother's mouth. Watching her mother's eyes widen to madness. Hearing her muffled attempt at screaming an order. Feeling her mother writhe underneath her.

"You told that principal, that Pam Grier looking bitch that you AGREED with her decision to suspend me."

The muffled screaming at her hand becomes more violent. Prompting her to remove it out of curiosity. To hear her victim's voice unimpeded. To listen to her mother's suffering in the twilight.

Ice

"Get off of me I can't BREATHE!"

Samantha feels her mother's fear. Flowing outward in the struggle Vibrating into her body.

"Get OFF!"

The mother screams this with the last ounce of her strength. Face stung red with the slap. Holding her head far back in the effort. Trying hard to push up and writhe out from under her daughter.

The daughter takes hold of her mother's arms. Easily pinning them to her sides. Watching her mother give away the last of her energy in a panic. Watching her hold her head far back, shaking it as she screams a deep, woman's scream. A scream hot with rage. Touched cold by fear. A swirling of emotional oblivion, until there is no more energy left to scream.

"You want me to get off?"

"Yes, PLEASE."

This syllable, given at the pitch of a siren, sung quiet in the new weakness of her spirit.

"Then take off your clothes."

"I will NOT."

The daughter struggles on top of her mother. Working to get her mother's arms pinned behind her back underneath her. Finding her mother's delicate fingers in the wake of it. Holding her mother there in authority. Asking, *"are you gonna get 'em off?"*

"NO!!"

And in the shadow of this, comes a deep, howling scream for the ages. A scream of agony unleashed.

"I'll take 'em off! I'll take 'em OFF!!"

Upon this feeling that courses through. The daughter rises up. Going across the bedroom and locking the door. Returning to her mother's side, to watch her closely. Watching her remove every stitch of clothing. Knowing when the woman bends over to slide her underwear down, watching the breasts swing and toll the like D Major key. Knowing from the fleshy, cinched in waist and heavy hips what must be.

In anger renewed, the girl walks fully clothed over to her mother's dresser. Finding the wooden hairbrush of legend.

"Oh, no you don't," the mother says, shaking her head no. *"I will not let you do this to me. I am still your MOTHER."*

"You will lay your FAT ASS across my knee," the girl says. *"Or I swear to God I will never FUCKING speak to you again!"*

In the wake of this fear. In the nightmarish afterthought of this terror. The humiliated woman lowers her arm from her breasts. Moving her hand from her front. Letting her body display itself in voluptuous curves and beauty. A face and neck remarkably free from the fleshiness of her curves. A woman's fully developed body, made more beautiful by the pretty face. A face somber in defeat. In emotional defiance.

She stares deeply into her daughter's eyes. Watching her daughter sit fully clothed in her jeans and button down blue shirt at the edge of the bed. Face somber in full, defiant emotion, the woman lies humiliated across her daughter's lap. Breasts hung down low in nakedness. Bottom in heart shaped nudity across her daughter's lap. Determined to take the punishment without sound. Without motion.

The first blow resounds through her flesh. Through her spirit. Opening her mouth in shock and disbelief. Never understanding the nature of fire. The nature of it when placed against the skin.

Ice

The second blow causes her to tense her bottom. Straining and breathing to remain quiet. Putting her hand over her already reddened backside.

"Get your hand down," her daughter says. *"Get your hand DOWN!"*

In angry determination, the mother complies. Placing her hands again obediently upon the floor. Feeling the daughter wrap her legs around hers. Holding her tight.

The next blow is the first of a series of hard, fast strikes of heat into her skin. A heat that grows from the point of origin, to reach down into her buttock with flaming sorcery. To grab stubbornness by the throat, and choke it to death. This heat and acid agony grows until the forty two year old woman's voice must comply. Until the mature voice must cry out in an involuntary yell, like that of a warrior woman in battle. A yell of defiance. The last barrier of resistance fallen away.

The daughter moves to the other side. To the other side of naked life on display. Turning the mother's white skin to blood. Relentlessly pounding the wooden hairbrush to both sides of her mother's big bottom. Focused. Determined. Hearing the warrior in her mother's voice begin to fade. Hearing the onset of a surrender in weeping.

The daughter sees the armor break. Seeing the skin go thin in one single place among the bruises. Signaled by instinct to finish here. Slamming the brush down upon the spot where blood hath appeared. Staining a touch of the paddling hairbrush wood to blood.

The daughter listens to her mother's defiance turn. Listening to the pain in her voice rise to weeping. Ceasing the hot paddling motion. Studying every bruised, bloody inch of her mother's bottom. Feeling her mother weep for mercy.

Samantha Daley rides the wind. Making Pricilla stand to her feet. Ordering her over to the mirror. Seeing her handiwork in voluptuous beauty and bruising as her mother walks. Marveling the trickle of blood formed.

The mother turns her backside to the mirror. Saying *oh my God,* when she sees her skin. Covering her face in epic humiliation. Her body shaken from the new sobbing nurtured and borne.

Her daughter sits quietly on the bed. Staring in control. In contempt.

Samantha Daley rides the wind. On the eve of eschatology.

My Daughter's

Kisses

20

My daughter's kisses are sweet to the palate. They flow into me through the tip of my tongue, ringing a chime to my ears and the back of my brain down to the core and center of my body and soul. I waste no further energy in self delusion, that yes, I am the culprit here—I am the one who hath perpetrated this lust, creating within her the motheress spirit, which affects the both of us when we are in proximity to one another. I find myself daydreaming of my daughter's naked body even now, when I am at the kitchen counter of my avocation, which is to turn this sweet batter in this silver mixing bowl into an angel food layer cake with pink icing. The simpler the cake recipe, the more I tend to like it, preferring the simplicity of yellow and lemon over carrot or red velvet. And I don't just bake these three layer cakes as a hobby, I *eat* them, which is why my bra and underwear are stuffed so mightily, which is rightfully so for a woman if she pleases. Every extra pound I gain goes straight to my breasts and hips, creating the unwanted hourglass of legend, which my daughter insists is 'too hot to handle.'

And even while I dip my finger into the ivory batter, followed by the full spoonful I cannot resist, I feel the sudden phantom tingle at these flower dressed hips of mine hidden, where the white dress cloth and midnight blue flower pattern hides the truth from spirit eyes that stare. This truth being in the form of our newest perversion just last night, where we explored a profoundly hip centered psychology, which had her on her knees behind me in the middle of the floor, me standing up in the nude, with my hand pressed perfectly still between my legs without moving at all, while she grabbed, squeezed, shook and jiggled my wide and wiggly bottom without ceasing, until I noticed the feeling inside my hips begin to flow toward where my hand was pressed at my groin. And I could not resist, as with this extra spoonful of sweet cake batter, the lifting up of one of my great, hanging breasts and pulling my own nipple into my mouth, nursing it as if thirsty to drink, until a triad of energy completed this spontaneous cycle, and I began to moan helplessly with my own breast sucked into my mouth, while my entire body shook like a jackhammer.

And I knew this was a unique orgasm in my life's corrupted history, guided into existence by the motheress spirit, and the feel of my daughter's hands kneeding the flesh at my backside. And I remember afterwards—as she kissed and licked every inch of it with a voracious hunger—having to steady myself from swooning, and make sure I did not allow the room to go spinning around.

This is the Daydream of Eve, that haunts my mind and body as I hear the door open and shut, and the object of my desire drifts across time and space, drawn upon the current of "Hi, Mom" toward the kitchen. And I can feel a spark of 'how-de-do,' hopped from my heart to the rest of my body, as the tallish, blonde girl with the deep blue eyes steps happily into my 3D space, stepping up behind me as I pour the batter—grabbing me by the waist and tickling my ribs—enough to make me laugh in fear and sorrow, as I struggle to hold on to the spoon and the silver mixing bowl. She has mercy on me though, planting one of her firm, full lipped kisses against my face from behind. *What a beauty,* my mind says to me, while I spoon the batter equally into the three round cake pans.

Then the tell-tale squeeze of her blue jean groin against my flower cloth dress reminds me instantly of last night, when she stood up against the back of me, taking hold of both my naked breasts and pressing her groin against my naked bottom. She had held me still, in the aftermath of trauma, until it was as though her body started to move on its own, slamming into me with hard, steady pelvic thrusts at least four seconds apart, a rhythm that her body would not let her break, until she suddenly could not pull back anymore, and the trumpet sound of her voice rung my ears while I felt every inch of her body tremble. Then after this trauma, she groaned and grunted her own amazement of this power, her legs twitching again in reminder, of what life and death struggle her body had just endured.

I am reminded of this, as her next kiss against my cheek is not pulled away, and I hear, I *feel* the strong breathing from her nose, then feel the grip of her hands, squeezing deeply into my breasts over the dress cloth, causing me to close my eyes in pure anguish and involuntary gratitude, having to let the bowl drop to the counter with the spoon slid down inside, buried completely into what batter doth still remain. I let my lips slide directly onto hers, feeling the instant touch of her tongue to the tip of mine, causing me to draw a deep breath as I turn, wrapping both arms around her neck in a lover's kiss, feeling her hands new over my dress at my backside hidden.

The taste of my daughter's kiss is sweet to my palate, to be sure, as a soft sugar cookie over a hard hunger, causing my body to shudder once unseen from head to toe. And suddenly, our kiss takes on a deeper power of its own volition, where our mouths are both open wide but locked together, our tongues probing deep inside, pressed, and mashed together in unison, to where we are unable to pull our mouths apart. Breathing loudly through our noses, my voice betraying a whimper as I feel her hands sliding my dress up in the back, giving a mighty squeeze to my hips, which causes me to grab her head with both hands to hold this strange kiss locked in position.

And I am suddenly tipped over the line of reasoning, when her hand slides to the front of me, under my white dress cloth, proceeding to rub me inside my underwear, which causes me to forget my own name, and have to hold onto this deep kiss for dear life, as my daughter obeys her inner command, and does her duty from the ages passed down east of Eden.

I hold on tight to this deep kiss, with her hand up the front of my dress, rubbing smoothly this steady rhythm, across the rapid wetness of this awakening, and the hardening of this proper place in time. She rubs her hand in this steady rhythm while I hold on, suddenly aware that this buildup of energy in my body will soon prove fatal to my feeble sanity, and I am suddenly tensed up in fear from head to toe.

Without mercy, she rubs me down below, in full command of the swollen nature of my pitiful desire uncovered, rubbing her mother's desperation as unto a calling, to serve what spirits that beckon. And from somewhere deep within, I am suddenly aware of my own mother's pitiful whimpering, and a mighty lurching of her hips in squeezing in the bedroom mirror of my youth, and the tension in my body breaks, sending the Amazonian grunt into my daughter's mouth, as I hold onto her head as I double over, while she lowers with me in the power of a deep understanding, holding the kiss as my grunting transforms to bellowing into her mouth, until I have to bend over far enough to make her understand that my body can endure no more.

On the edge of this rebel yell, I stand in the aftermath of trauma, hugged up tight against my daughter, breathing deeply as she rubs my back, unable to remember the layers of angel food cake on the counter, and whether or not one or two of the three layers were poured to completion.

21

*W*hat breast centered psychology hath returned to my tragic need, here in the rains of this November wind? Ever since my daughter came home that day, and molested me at the angel food cake counter, the feel of my own mother's breasts in my mouth have dominated my soul's memory. For it is the flash of my mother's orgasm at the bedroom mirror of my youth that finally triggered my Angel Food Orgasm, when I saw her hips squeeze into oblivion on their own. I remember it had happened because I had been inspired, even at age 13, to reach down while I was rubbing her, and pull one of the great breasts into my mouth at the nipple, clumsily losing suction of the heavy thing in my weak little lips, watching it fall heavily back into place against her body. And even though I had stopped rubbing her for a brief moment, holding my hand perfectly still, I felt with my other hand her hips tense up violently, and her whole body did the Armageddon Quake against her will, while she foolishly strained not to make a sound, causing the energy in her voice to build up, and escape from her mouth in a hideous shriek for the ages.

My mother's orgasms were very powerful. Brought on primarily by stimulation of her breasts, whether it be by massage or nursing, oftentimes to full completion, where no other stimulation beyond this was necessary to push her over the edge. When I was 13, I had nursed her breasts so much that the milk was hardly a surprise when it came, which was merely the completion of our erotic circle at the time, that we were privileged to the sweet taste of the forbidden.

Forbidden fruit is the sweetest taste to the palate. And maybe this is why Lucy was never so completely out in the open as I am with Miranda, never taking her breasts out for this pleasure unless it was behind a locked door, and sometimes with the lights out. It was nothing for her to have me laid across her lap in a dark bedroom for the better part of a half hour at her milky breast, nursing her until she had to breathe deeper and sit up straighter, in anticipation of what was going to happen. For my mother, the fumbling of my clumsy hands at her shirt was foreplay; my feeble attempts to unlatch her bra bore the power of a kiss, and the pulling of her nipple into my mouth had the energy of a hand at her groin.

Whether or not this was something my bygone father ever knew of her, this I do not know. But I am burdened by the spirits of motherline knowledge, and the tributaries of it that flow through every woman, knowing that my mother's older sister certainly knew it, and carried it through my mother's life from the same age of 13, the age where this was passed down to me.

I am in my daughter's lap of depravity now. On of all places...the bathroom toilet, both of us stark naked, watching this seventeen year old beauty service my corruption so hungrily, sucking the nipples so skillfully back and forth, building such a powerful frustration in me, because she refuses to stay on one long enough. The scent of Lucy's depravity is still strong in my nostrils, when I remember us behind the locked doors of the little bathroom in the small white house, with my 13 year old self in her lap facing her, pulling on her nipples with both hands, while her cheeks are sunk in from the sucking at my undeveloped little B cups, bellowing loudly through her nose, from the power of what a stool softener is designed to do.

And I know that these taboos will remain such, until the Second Coming, as the revelation of them cannot be accepted by the spirit of hypocrisy, nor can the endtime truth that woman is wayward, and is heavy laden with burdens of the unspeakable.

Of this deep and darkest depravity, I can feel it being sucked to life by my daughter as I sit in her lap, not facing her but turned to the side, both my legs closed, rubbing her big globes as she gently sucks mine one by one. Her tongue back and forth on my nipple, while it is pulled into her mouth activates my body and my soul's memory, to my mother's depravity behind the locked bathroom door when I was 13, with her mouth wide open and vacuum clamped at my breasts, moving back and forth between them in madness, with me straddled on her lap facing her—watching her stop just long enough to focus on one of them...

When she does this in my body's recollection, I am forced to say to my daughter *"put this one in your mouth, baby,"* telling her to *"please keep it there,"* and to pull it as deep into her mouth as she can, sliding up and down on it without ceasing. Upon this, the sound of my mother's insanity vibrates my soul's memory, where I can feel her gruff, animal groaning onto my young breast again, while the stool medicine takes effect on her body a second time, behind the locked door of our little bathroom.

I watch my daughter engage the Virgin's Intercourse, feeling my mother upon it from somewhere else along the timeline, until I can hear the breathing in my thirteen year old self give way, to the sound of a pitiful young siren, accompanied by the blast of my soul's fervent siren call in the present day.

Fear and Loathing

22

*T*he rains of November continue to fall, in the wake of threats and intimidation on Miranda and Emily's tranquility. They have taken to themselves in the crowd of nothings and wannabes, the crowd of kings and queens, princes and princesses at the school, no longer afraid to be labeled and ridiculed as *those two dyke witches* by everybody on campus that matters, led by Samantha Daley and her terrible trio, none of whom have missed the opportunity to stop and stare at them when they walk by, sometimes even giving that fearful, universal sign of some terrible tragedy impending, which is the finger across the front of the throat. But the truth is, when my daughter told me these things, the worry in my heart turned not to my daughter's safety. Somehow already…I know better.

My mind is adrift in tragedy upon the four winds, where I can see two lonely figures in the November rain, walking together in the colors of their hearts' burden, one in a cloak as black as the raven strands of hair, the other in cloth as gray as these rainy skies under the hidden Forest Moon.

The late afternoon rainfall attacks the two of them as they walk slowly together, both well protected under the huge black umbrella. They walk down the empty pathway through the neighborhood park, undeterred by the wind and driving rainfall, nor the deadly swishing of the branches along the nearby pine forest, and the blowing of dead leaves from the leaf bearing trees gone dead for another winter.

The two of them walk on in the glory of Fate. Having been blessed to find one another in this cold wilderness, where they have been touched by the warmth of genuine understanding, and the comfort of compassion and empathy.

The two of them take refuge out of the rain, underneath the park shelter, kept safe by the wet, weeping world—from the busybodying crowd of pleasure seekers, and those bound by the spirit of *fungalooga* in the latter day.

"They did it to me again today," Emily says.

"What?"

"Hand across the throat. Samantha did it while Jenny just looked at me like she felt sorry for me. You know how she does. That 'I'm sorry you have to die' look."

"Jenny Lynn Johnson should be ashamed of herself. I think she knows better, but she's trapped by those girls. She's a prisoner of everything they say. Everything they do. Even the black girls are scared of them."

"I know. Ever since Samantha beat Billy Coe on the mat, remember? And he outweighs her by like 20 pounds. She's won Jiu jitsu and Judo tournaments, you know. And now the whole school knows it."

"Did you see it?"

"I heard about it. She jumped up and wrapped her legs around his neck. They said he hit the mat like a rag doll and she held her legs around his throat until he was almost unconscious. They had to pull her off him because he wouldn't give up. It's just what I heard, I don't know if it's true. Are you scared?"

As if in grieving to answer, the winds draw their attention to the blowing of trees nearby, followed by the rock and rolling of several pine cones tossed from the big pine tree nearby, falling from their invisible place on the shelter roof to the ground. Emily watches her blonde soulmate stand up in her long, charcoal gray coat, wandering out into the rain for just enough seconds to grab the largest pine cone she sees.

Emily stares in mild confusion, brushing a strand of brunette hair from over her eyes. Miranda returns to her place at their barren, November picnic table, the two of them facing out into the November storm of wind and rain. Miranda holds the huge pine cone upright in the palm of her hand, causing Emily's unspoken bewilderment to grow.

What lesson in fear and loathing, is there to be learned from the lowly pine cone, plucked by the winds from a November tree?

Emily Watson suddenly feels the cool breath at her lips drawn in, to fill her lungs with the breath of life, as she watches the earthen brown mystery begin to form a coat of snow white crystal upon itself from the bottom to the top, until it is transforms from wooded plainness, into the beauty of frosted crystal and snowy white.

"God and Holy *Jesus*… are you a real witch?"

Emily takes the crystal pine cone away from her blonde queen, staring in shock and disbelief, at what looks as though it were carved out of pure ice.

"Throw a pine cone to the concrete," she says, "and it'll bounce like a dry sponge. But if I throw this…"

"No… please don't," Miranda says, holding Emily's wrist. Gently. "Please don't."

"Oh my God your hand… your hand is cold as *ice.*" She looks on in awestruck wonder, as her friend takes her little work of art from her, and places it gently on the table. Emily moves her head closer. Staring into the eyes of winter blue.

"Are you a *witch?*"

Miranda sighs, looking out at the cold rain attacking the concrete walkway in the nearby distance.

"I don't know," she says.

"But… I mean… how long have you been able to do it? And… what *is* it?"

"Since I was a little girl," she says. "One day I was playing in the snow. I was packing a snowman, and I noticed that I could move the snow without touching it. Like I could brush it off with an invisible tool. I kept doing this until I was able to carve the snow into shapes. I even started to make a little snow girl that appeared in my mind. Then my Mom showed up and I stopped."

"Does she know? Does she know what you can do?"

"She knows."

"Well, what did she say?"

She told me she understood and then she fucked me…

"Mom's great about it. She's a beautiful person. I want you to meet her soon."

"If I could do something like that," Emily says, "my Mom would beat my ass like a pack mule until I learned how to do tricks with it that would make her rich."

"I know you're just joking," Miranda says, smiling a little. Until she sees Emily look away, as if gazing into the heart of a disturbing memory.

"I wish I were. But forget about me. You're a real life *Frozen.* An actual *freak.*"

Miranda's shocked, slightly hurt stare makes Emily put her hands over her own mouth in apology. "Oh my God I didn't mean that. I just meant that what I saw is so incredible nobody would believe it. People would think it was a trick even if they saw it with their own eyes. Hey, do me a favor... freeze another one of those things..."

Emily hurries out into the rain, grabbing the first pine cone she can get her hands on, one half the size and beauty of the first one. She hands the smaller, misshapen thing to Miranda, watching in renewed, rapt amazement as it turns into a crystalline thing in like loveliness as the first. Emily takes it, grabs it from her, and smashes it to the concrete floor below, covering her mouth with both hands again, staring down at the infinity of crystal shards scattered at their feet.

With the umbrella in one hand, and the ice cold hand of her friend in the other, Emily pulls Miranda hurriedly across the open park lawn, to where a tree about as tall as a two story house stands with nearly every dead leaf blown or washed away. Without saying a word to her blonde companion, she points at the scraggly, November tree—standing by confidently, holding their umbrella up high, as Miranda touches both hands to the trunk.

And though she thought she was prepared for the sight, the next minute of her life is spent in breathless wonder, as she watches the autumn tree transform before her eyes in the rain, becoming a tree from somewhere along the timeline, with every branch covered in a layer of frozen rain and icicles hanging down.

"Now I know," Emily says, the single tear betraying her soul's revelation.

"What?"

Emily looks away from the Autumn landscape's new, icy warning. Staring into the eyes of blue and winter.

"Now I know... why you're not afraid of them."

The death of Indian Summer haunts the November landscape in a grieving mist, until it seems that the entire earth is covered in a cold, misty rain. The students at West Amber high school are adrift in the pain of this post Halloween malaise, lost somewhere on the road to Thanksgiving, and another brief respite from their perpetual misery. Miranda and Emily mingle and drift as two lonely flowers in a meadow of tall grasses—looking, feeling more conspicuous and out of place than ever. Becoming inseparable, trying to spend as many minutes of the day together as they are allowed. Protecting each other from the growing storm of negativity, from the constant buildup of dark energy flowing from the beautiful, elite girls of the school, until the two of them are unable to pass by them without protecting their emotions, looking down or away in silent submission—enduring whatever cruel remarks there may be, or sometimes a quiet, sinister stare, or a burst of eruptive, explosive laughter. For many weeks, through the passing of Indian Summer, and the arrival of All Hallows Eve, they have perpetuated the cloud of vicious rumor, and the rise of fear in the hearts of the lonely.

This bell chimes the closing of another hour of suffering. Calling the students forth from their classroom prisons to the empty hallways, which are soon filled with scores of young tragedies in the making. Girls and boys in the bodies of young men and women, some having already matured into deep adulthood in both mind and body alike. Drifting in this daily eight hour prison, so many of them burned out already on life even before it has begun. The beautiful and the unbeautiful, the talented and the untalented, the lucky and the unlucky among them—every clique and cliché ever imagined in the heart and soul of youth, all rushing to their lockers to exchange whatever books and notebooks there may be, among them one pale, brunette beauty who stops alone at the fateful locker, where the beginning of the end first came to life, many long weeks ago.

The shy brunette pushes one book into the locker, pulling another one free, unaware of the familiar wave that approaches.

"Where's your dyke friend, Witch Hazel?"

This, spoken with vigor and venom, followed by their laughter erupted, loud enough to make everyone nearby stop what they were doing and stare.

"You know what? *Fuck* you, Samantha."

Suddenly, their line of four is like a truck jackknifed across the highway, with the Samantha cab slamming on its brakes with tires squealing, with the other three as the trailer, careening to the side across the road.

"What did you say?" Samantha says, walking slowly toward the goth girl in a fog of genuine disbelief.

"You heard me. I said *fuck* you."

The pain of an inner lightning strike twists Samantha's bewilderment into a rage unleashed, causing her to literally wince from it, her hand striking out like a hungry cobra to Emily's poor neck, slamming her against the locker with a loud bang, both their books flying off to the floor, somewhere near their feet. They all watch as the brunette grabs the blonde's arm in a hopeless effort, feeling the pressure locking in around her neck, to make her breathing harder with each passing second.

And somewhere in the haze of motion, she sees the strong girl's other hand in a clinched fist raised, then grabbed at the last moment by Rosalyn Reynolds, helped along by the beautiful Kelly LeMonde, with Jennifer Johnson prying the girl's grip from around her neck. Emily feels the scratching claw at her throat pulled away, watching the three girls grab full hold of the school's head cheerleader, holding onto her as she begins to writhe and pull against them in near madness, as if getting back to the goth girl at the locker were something that her life depended on.

"You fucking dyke *bitch!* Let me go…let me get my hands around her fucking throat! I'm gonna fucking kill you witch! You fucking dyke *cunt!* I'm gonna fucking *kill you!!"*

And every nearby student and teacher watches the scene as dumbfounded; mesmerized by the sight of the school beauty, the school rich girl and the school bully all rolled into one being dragged away like an unruly mental patient, down the hall and through an open door to a half empty classroom, the students inside looking on in nervous awe as the three pretty girls hold their beautiful mistress as tight as they can. Rosalyn holds her tight with her arm around Samantha's neck, while the other two hold both her arms immobile, while she jerks, screams and bellows like an animal to get away. They hold her there still, for the better part of a full minute while she breathes and moans, Rosalyn finally able to move her arm from around her neck and rub her head, whispering something in her ear to calm her down further, as she continues to breathe deeply from the trauma, and the tears roll down her face in quiet anger and weeping.

The earth flows along the plane of the ecliptic, on its blue path among the stars, spinning from one hour to the next, in the cover of ashen gray regret. Beneath these clouds of grieving, somewhere in the aftermath of trauma, the four horsemen of this apocalypse languish together in the throes of end of the world hunger and thirst, in the comfort cushioned booth of pizza parlor luxury.

"The problem is we've waited too long," Rosalyn says, sipping her red glass Coke through a straw. "I told you we should have gotten her ass at Halloween."

Samantha swallows her irritation in a gulp of Mt. Dew. The icy cold burns her throat beautifully with every swallow.

"I wasn't feeling it at Halloween," she says. "Besides, I doubt she would have fallen for it anyway. She would have never come to our party dressed as a *witch.* "

"Oh, yes she would have. She's too *stupid* and pathetic not too. I guarantee you, she's dying inside to be one of us. To be our friend. For us to be nice to her goth ass."

"She's got Miranda now," Kelly says, lightly sipping her drink. "She doesn't need us anymore."

"What the Hell is it with Miranda anyway? She was alright last year. And this year, she's just fucking weird."

"And she looks different too," Kelly says. "I think she bleached her hair or something. I don't remember her being *that* blonde."

"Or that beautiful," Jennifer chimes in, her lips wrapped around her Coke straw, refusing to risk the eye contact.

"Beautiful?" Samantha says. "She looks like a fucking giraffe."

Rosalyn nearly chokes on her soda, from the laughter formed on its own. The 'Afrodite' goddess tattoo on her upper arm rests hidden under her black coat.

"I don't see why I have to do anything to her," Jennifer says. "Emily's always been— "

"Because you're gonna do whatever the Hell I *tell* you to do, that's why," Samantha says. Glaring at Jennifer like an abusive mother over a bitchy daughter. The other two gaze at Jenny Lynn quietly. Without sympathy.

"You gotta admit it though." Jennifer says. "She did *something* over the summer."

"Yeah," Kelly says. "Breast implants, contacts and a bleach job."

"Now why would she get breasts implants," Jennifer says boldly.

"How else can you explain the size of her tits? I know they didn't get that big naturally. She looks ridiculous."

"And her eyes weren't that blue last year," Samantha says. "And her hair wasn't that blonde either."

"So, basically you're saying she's fake," Kelly says.

"As a silk flower. She might look good, but she's not real."

"But why did she do it?" Rosalyn asks, her face burdened by genuine confusion. "I mean, she was already pretty. Now she just looks… weird."

"Look, who cares," Samantha says. "Forget about Miranda. That frosty cunt isn't the problem anyway. At least, not yet. The problem is the bastards and bitches that think we're playing games. Starting with that fat assed, fat breasted Pam Grier looking bitch of a principal. I told you that what we've got planned for her is gonna make history. And that's gonna happen *so* much sooner than later, trust me."

Samantha Daley takes a long, plaintive sip of her Coke. Allowing for that great looking away. To where her eyes are suddenly trained toward a place beyond the ceiling of their little outing, to somewhere in the cold mist of autumn rain, even above the covering of gray clouds and misery.

"Forget about everything you thought you knew," she says, leaning intimately toward the other three's company and attention. "Forget about what you thought you understood. The time for playing games is over. Enough of the hypocrisy. The pretense. There are those who don't understand that what you know is nothing in this life. And that *who* you know is everything…

"The straight and narrow is for losers. Being a goody two shoes is for suckers. If you want something out of life, you have to *take* it. Do whatever you need to do, until you have it in the palm of your hands. And to Hell with anything, and any*body* who gets in your way."

The four of them lean forward towards the center of their energy, as if drawn to a calling, to the revelation of their immediate future impending.

"That nigger bitch principal… is going to cry. Then that witch bitch *dyke*… is going to die."

Samantha Daley's voice is low.

Almost whispery.

Jonathan Lovejoy

Haddie May Greer Rides the Wind

Haddie May Greer rides the wind. On the eve of eschatology.

Hadly Elizabeth Howard. Haddie May Howard. The four 'B's of latter day womanhood in tow. From the teenage years through Columbia University. Through the Master's Degree in English Literature. Brains. Beauty. Breasts. Buttocks. With the fifth B thrown in for good measure. Breeding.

Haddie May Greer rides the wind. On the eve of eschatology.

Possessing an even greater beauty than the famed actress she is accused of resembling. The world's first cinematic super heroine. This foxy brown beauty she bears the slightest likeness to, only a lighter, more golden shade of beauty. Having not even been told she looks like this actress, until she married her white husband Tom Greer.

Haddie May Howard. Haddie May Greer. Daughter of a black physician. A white female professor. Having cruised through life on a memory bestowed. Cursed with a love of reading. A gift for test taking. A brilliant memory, masquerading as intellect. Shining like a light in darkness. Glowing like a white rose among weeds.

She's the best principal we've ever had, they say. Keeping the students in check. Having a run of power and control among these latter day boys and girls. Keeping the privileged among them in their place.

Haddie May steps in golden skinned beauty through the mist. Alone in the school parking lot this Friday afternoon. Content to leave another week behind, in the shadows of her past. To look forward to an impending return to the Ivy League someday, to receive her PhD in English Literature. Having already hob knobbed with the Princeton elite. Having already shined the four 'B's in their faces. Having already blinded their unspoken hypocrisy to oblivion. White teethed, bright eyed complacency.

In the mist of a November rain. In the parking lot of West Amber High School. Haddie May Greer feels a crossing over. The beginning of the end of time, when the door of silver Infinity luxury opens, and a hand grabs her wrist tight.

She turns to see a black masked face. With a place to display eyes of beauty.

Before she can open her mouth to speak. Another hand reaches from behind her head. Holding her immobile. Then a third set of hands. Smaller, weaker hands. Three sets of hands, these are. Pushing her into the back seat of the car. Holding her down in violence, these two. Now, two sets of hands, they are. Holding the strong, beautiful principal in the back seat. Tearing at her clothes as the car cranks.

Two sets of beautiful eyes in the front of her privileged space. Two sets of hands at her body in the back. Holding her down. Punching her in the ribs. Holding her over her mouth. Pressing down hard on her. Forcing her to lie on her back in her own car being driven.

Haddie May rides the wind. The winds of November fear and pain. Being allowed to speak and yell loudly in the space of the car. To demand where she is being taken. To claim the ability to see through those 'weak little masks,' she says. To claim that she knows who at least one of them is.

In the mist of this Virginia tragedy. In the rains from Melancholy Bay. The voice nearest Haddie's face says. *"Hold this bitch tight."*

In the wake of these words spoken, the eyes of beauty look at the breasts of privilege. Big, flopping breasts of beauty. A set of hands, raising the black mask just above feminine lips. Lips pursed with inner rage. Lips tight with a merciless anger. These lips are open, when the black masked head lowers down. Biting the privileged woman's breasts through her bra. Listening to her scream in rage and pain.

Haddie May Greer rides the wind. On the eve of eschatology.

Are you gonna shut the fuck up? The voice of strength and beauty says. In the wake of her defiance, she feels her breast bitten again. A longer, more severe bite this time. A bite that draws a spot of blood through the woman's bra. Absorbing the precious spit into the cloth. Cushioning the breast from whatever mark that may tell.

Somewhere outside of Richland Hills, Virginia. Among the forests and fields of isolation. The silver Infinity is parked in the grass and weeds of November. Nearby the evergreen forest trees of Autumn.

In the back seat of rolling luxury stood still, the middle aged, light skinned beauty has every stitch of her clothing ripped and torn away. This, to the music of threats, screams, and pleading. Big, heavy, yellow breasts flopped beyond dignity. Big, brown areolas and nipples exposed in cold and pain. Arms handcuffed behind her back as she pleads, being held up against the back seat by two. Having to plead in sorrow, when she sees the big, realistic member exposed from black pants unzipped and lowered down. Hearing the vulgar nightmare spoken: *Hold this bitch up so I can fuck her.* Seeing a pair of white, feminine hands raise up their own black turtleneck shirt. Seeing those same hands raise their own bra up just enough. Seeing two high, rounded, white breasts jutting forward in waiting. Feeling her own breasts pulled up, and pressed against the white breasted demon. Feeling the demon's nipples jutting into hers. Understanding that fear can create arousal in the body. Understanding the nature of curses passed down. Of principalities through the generations, and of what motherline sins must be paid for in full.

At the door of her chastity. She feels the strapped on member pushed in. Unable to draw a breath through her own open mouth as it happens. Feeling the little world around her become a haze of twisted reality. A space of roving darkness settled in. Feeling the death of herself happen at the center of her life. Feeling the burn of blue and black fire.

Haddie May feels the onset of the Amazonian aura. The power of Testros, as it flows through Estros herself. The masculine channeled through the feminine. Feeling this white girl demon holding on, thrusting into her in latter day commitment. The energy of a moving train unleashed. Slamming like the piston of a luxury cruise ship from a century before. Slamming into her without mercy. Deep up inside her without pity.

The handcuffed woman feels the rise of tension in her captor's body. Feeling her movements take a mind of their own. Slamming the girl's body forward in a rhythm neither fast nor slow. A rhythm unique in the annals of time. Uniquely placed at the end of human history.

The privileged woman hears the onset of death. The death of her captor's sanity. Hearing the rise of a spirit voice. The voice of Amazonia's arrival. The siren call of the Saphhic volcano. The endtime trump of God unleashed.

This spirit torments the captor's body into agony. Making her draw a breath, to bellow another bovine call into the tiny space around them. Her body shaking the Armageddon Quake. Her spirit trembling with the end of the age born and bred.

Hattie May Greer rests there. Her back against the back cushion seat of luxury. Feeling the aftermath of trauma in the girl's body. Hearing her breathe to recover. Feeling her breathe to live again.

In the mist of an autumn rain. In the lonely outskirts of isolation. The woman blinks the rest of the tears from her eyes. The rest of the trauma from her soul.

Hattie May Greer rides the wind. On the eve of eschatology.

The Current of Melancholy Truth

"I've got such a bad feeling about things."

Emily stands the window of her bedroom, her attention suddenly drawn out into the Autumn wind and rain.

"And the funny thing is, it's like the more scared I get, the worse this storm gets. Maybe, I *am* a witch."

Miranda looks up from her math homework, her head turned toward Emily's last comment in enigmatic concern.

"Those girls really do have power," Emily says. "It's no bullshit. Somehow, they actually run the school. Somebody could write a freaking book about it and call it "The Six Degrees of Samantha Daley." Because it seems that everybody in the whole school is somehow connected to her in some major or minor way. Remember that Freshman cheerleader who broke her arm at the beginning of the year?"

"Barely, but yeah. I *do* remember."

"I was in the bathroom stall, when I heard two of Samantha's friends talking about it. I'll never forget it because I made it a point to keep my mouth shut and not make a sound while they were talking. It's a miracle they didn't discover me, because they thought the bathroom was empty. I was afraid that if they found me in there... well, I actually got up onto the toilet from the floor, just in case they looked under the stall. My heart was beating so fast. Thank God they didn't look in that stall. I heard them say that Brenda Francis, the girl with the broken arm, had been acting 'too big for her britches,' whatever that means, and that she was '*lucky that all she got out of it was a broken arm. Next time she opens her fucking mouth to one of us she'll think twice about it.*'"

"Are you saying that those girls broke her arm?"

"I saw this Brenda girl at the water fountain just a few days ago. I couldn't resist talking to her. She's two years younger than me and she's as tall as *you* are already. And I said "*How's your arm?*" She said "*Oh, fine, thanks for asking,*" and then she laughed for some reason like it tickled her. God, she looks like she was created in a lab or something. She freakishly perfect looking. And I asked her how it happened. She said it was an accident. It happened when she was practicing a routine. "*They threw me up but they didn't catch me when I came down,*" she said, then she laughed again and that was it. She left."

"So what does that have to do with Samantha and her friends?"

"You know that black girl Shondra? The girl who's locker is beside mine? Well, the four horsemen were walking past us, and Shondra looked at them and said to me *'They are some scary assed bitches.'* Then she said *'You know they broke that girl's arm? That real pretty freshman cheerleader? The one that's as pretty as ALL of them?'* And I said—*'I talked to her. Her name is Brenda, and she said it was an accident.'* And Shondra said *'That's the bullshit she's telling everybody. My sister is best friends with one of the freshman cheerleaders. And the truth is they invited Brenda over to Samantha's house to supposedly practice with the varsity cheerleaders. And she got Brenda locked in one of them Judo moves, or whatever the fuck it was',* Shondra said, *'in the back yard until she broke her arm. But Brenda's telling everybody it happened during one of them high throwing moves they do."*

Emily looks away from the weeping world outside her window, to see what cataclysm the third part of the truth hath wrought.

"And there it is," she says. "The same look on your face I know I had. When Shondra told me the truth."

Satisfied that her job is done, Emily dismisses her friend's drained, distant expression without pity, turning back to the world's dismal, dreary acknowledgement of her misery.

And suddenly, the unseen force holding the numbers and equations together in Miranda's head dissipates, causing her to have to abandon this part of her meaningless academic travail. Pushing the so-called college level math book aside, Miranda slides off the homework bed, and drifts the current of melancholy truth over to her friend at the window. Without a word, she turns her grieving companion toward her, their gaze locked by an energy inexpressible, hearkened from the reality that the types of fear are many, and uniquely distinguished.

Miranda leans her friend's head against her shoulder. Gently stroking her hair in feeble comfort, gazing out the window at the drowning mist, the wet, weeping world... and its latter day bereavement under the hidden Forest Moon.

Jonathan Lovejoy

Amazon Mountain

At their window of grieving, the blonde queen blinks eyes of blue. Touching the suffering beauty upon her chin, lifting just enough, so that brown eyes can stare into eyes of icy blue.

"You're a real life goddess," Emily says. "And you have been so nice to me."

These words flow upon the current of grief, along with the single tear born from the brunette's eye, moving in such determination, such purpose down her face in a slow, steady stream. In the aftermath of this pain, the blonde lowers her lips to the dark haired girl, to push through the last of what pretense they have left, pushing both lips to hers in full, not allowing her to take a second breath through her mouth—pushing this full lipped kiss to her in aggression, while taking firm hold of both her friend's wrists, to make her understand the early fullness of what must be.

This is the motheress spirit born. The private love and lust of what must be.

And in the wake of this, she moves her kiss to the girl's neck, leading in with the full licking of the tongue, to cause the girl to draw in a heavy breath, and acknowledge the name of the God of Creation. Amidst the shimmer and shudder newly arisen, the blonde goddess slides the girl's sweater off over her head, making quick work of the buttons of her white blouse, to show the modest B cup cloth beneath the surface, and the promise of what torments the heart of desire. She slides the girl's shirt and long black skirt away, kissing the front of her creamy smooth thighs down to the knee, having mercy upon her grieving immolation, to pretend not to notice the profound twitch of her leg from top to bottom.

As the brunette stands exposed, still and cold in her bra and underwear, the blonde stands up in the fullness of her calling, in the power of what beauty she commands, sliding out of her sweater which is the blue of the bird's autumn feathers, then begins to undo the buttons of her sky blue blouse, fully prepared for what mountain of awe must accompany the brunette's fervent stare. She slides out of her sky blue shirt, to the melody of her friend's shock and disbelief, of what is possible in the power of the Almighty's touch on Creation.

And in the wake of this, the blonde reaches back, and unlatches the fettered bra cloth, to slide the cups pitched up somewhere nearby and beyond the phantom chord above G Major, to cause her friend to lose her ability to breathe, or to unlock her eyes from the beauty of Creation east of Eden.

The brunette stands there. Only able to stare as the gargantuan breasts are naked. Standing there, as they move forward to her own bra cloth, to collide with the lesser worlds they are, which makes the blonde beauty close her eyes, and hold her head back to rapture. She opens her eyes in renewed purpose, sliding her jeans away, unaware of the extreme nature of her own femininity in the brunette's vision, and the apocalyptic hanging of her bosom as she bends over.

She stands up again, in only her small, tight underwear cloth, touching her teeth and tongue to the brunette's naked shoulders, sliding down the bra straps from their doomed place of rest, reaching behind her to unlatch the fettered cloth from its bygone purpose and calling. She pulls the bra from its proper place, letting it fall unseen to the floor, unable to stop herself from grabbing hold of the girl's underwear, pulling it firmly down and away.

And she is unable to avoid fertility's call on her way back up, sliding her hands around the brunette's hips to the back, employing a mighty squeeze, staring at the front of her, in grieving to taste the fruit of what forbidden powers may be. She slides her hands past the wide and rounded hip spread, past the deep, inward waist curve, standing up in full power again, in the power of her easy command, staring at the helpless brunette girl, who is only able to look on in nervous uncertainty, waiting for what end of the world cataclysm this may be.

The blonde takes one of the globing globes in her hand, pushing the nipple firmly to the nipple of the young girl, the nipple of the teenage woman, rubbing it softly, firmly, softly, then firmly again, never rescuing her friend with even as much as a glance of reassurance, but gauging only the hardening of her friend's nipple, and her new attempt to hold her breathing in control. *"I think I'm gonna cum,"* the girl says, followed by the touching upon the Creator's name again, as the blonde girl rubs her nipple to her friend's without mercy, hearing her call to the name of Heaven again, as the energy builds a steady power in her voice, to flow out in a trembling that quivers her body from head to toe. The brunette stands firm, in the midst of her soul's confusion, as the fearful wave trembles her voice ad nauseam, as though her body were imprisoned by the hand of ice and cold.

And in the current of this wave come and gone, the nippling blonde reaches down and pulls her friend's nipple into her mouth, to cause a mighty spasm, and a fevered grunting of her friend's voice in trauma. From this, the blonde takes her tongue to the girl's neck, to lick and taste all of it, ending with her tongue at the girl's suffering lips, and a kiss born again of sensual force and power.

And the brunette gathers her breath and vision the best she can, holding on, suspended above this new plateau, feeling herself escorted over to the bed of this hope and dream, feeling herself adrift upon the wind of this Predestiny, laid out upon her back by the flow of this desire, and the birth of this unbearable new place in reality. She watches as the busty, blonde beauty brings her breasts down to hers again, sliding them down her body, past the naval in trembling, at last touching her hands to the proper place, to the brunette's improper place, gripping it firmly with her thumb and forefinger, squeezing it, moving it just enough to sustain this new arousal, staring down into the face of womanhood uncovered, to observe the truth of bygone innocence, and the beginning of the end of chastity in the soul.

She reaches down with her lips in readiness, to at last taste the power of this fruit forbidden, and the sweetness of bitter wormwood in the midst of paradise. She pulls the brunette's chastity into her mouth in one full, deep sucking, to cause the girl's body to tense from top to bottom, as she grabs the blonde by the hair, in feeble hope and prayer of keeping her there. But without mercy, with no pity formed and given, she moves her head away, pushing her breast up to this place of new grieving, placing the nipple at the top of the brunette's arousal, rubbing the nipple again with skill and power—seeing the girl stare down at her in shock and disbelief, at the rising of her body's feeling again, and her impending fall from the heights of ecstasy to oblivion.

And she rubs her nipple to the tip of this arousal with vigor. Hearing the girl's voice begin to moan in resistance, which is the edge of reluctance, which is the edge of fear. The blonde listens to this moan begin, watching the girl's arousal against her nipple grown to alarming size and strength, to where the glory of the *girlcock* is displayed— watching the girl have to writhe her hips just enough, until she has to sweetly admonish her to lie still, and accept the tragedy of what is about to happen to her body.

And in the near wake of this sweetness and power, the brunette perceives the gripping of a spirit around her mind and body, to dive her over the edge of this mountain cliff, to fall her to breathless speed and fear, causing her voice to do the siren call of Amazon Mountain, and the fall from the heights of the Amazonian plateau. She draws a second breath, lying still in obedience, feeling the rest of her flight from Heaven to Earth, followed by her body's shaking—by the quaking, the end of the world breaking of this new tension, causing her to grab onto the blonde and hold on for dear life, pushing herself up into her breast as hard as she can, in hopes of cushioning herself in this tragic fall from grace to glory.

Ice

She holds on to the blonde, her entire body tense with force and pushing, pushing her groin up into the blonde's bosom, feeling the blonde lower her lips to her bosoms on fire, to pull them both in the cool of her lips, giving them both a powerful sucking one by one, to complete the circle of desire between the two of them.

And the two of them lay there for this brief repose, at this moment in time. Breathing the aftermath of trauma, the brunette's legs wrapped up and around her, until the blonde can endure no more of her own body's waiting. She slowly slides her way to the final kiss of her body's tension, sliding her lower self to the brunette's place down below, her own body twitching from this new touch, sliding, searching, slipping herself into this perfect place—learning what rhythm, what melody of motion must be played to bring this sweet symphonic finale to life.

She pins her lover's arms to her sides. Pumping her in Amazonian missionary, finding the rhythm from the Curse of Nod, where the body's motion is uniquely wrought, and the ability to stop has come and gone. Powered by this drug, by this craving, her hips find this perfect pumping motion, her head down beside her victim, her own mouth hung open in anticipation, fearful of what she may have to endure in the rise and fall.

And she perceives the power of a new spirit, that tells her *don't change your rhythm when it happens*, and she feels the birth of this power in her groin; to spread heat through to her buttocks and up to her breasts, amidst the sound of her own voice bellowing deeply, accompanied by a high pitched soprano shriek from the brunette held tightly underneath her.

In the Midst

of Paradise

29

I remember my journey to Pilate Mountain

When my soulmate met me on the evening rim

We danced our Heart's Melody on the starlight trail

With pity in our hearts for God's judgment of them

30

In the grieving twilight rain, the two of them languish together in Emily's early evening bedroom, both having been caressed to sleep in the aftermath of trauma. Emily having lost her Amazonian chastity, having given away her virginity as it is possible without penetration, devastated by her body's complete and total annihilation times three. The cataclysm of their love has left them both spent, the two of them naked in each other's arms under the covers, adrift on a current of melancholy dreaming, where end of the world prophecies torment their sleep in blood, fire and vapor of smoke.

And somewhere in the flow of this eschatological dream, Emily envisions the two of them astroll in tranquility, among the grasses of a prairie meadow, nearby a forest grove of leafy green trees, where suddenly, she is shocked by the slithering of serpent green upon one of the branches, and the revelation of danger lurking in the midst of paradise. Then from the brushy confines of the forest grove, bursts an angry grizzly bear of profound rage doubled, in a threat to kill and devour the both of them.

Emily awakes with this proverbial start, snapping her head up from her lover's bosom, gazing into the twilight dark as though this dream animal might become real, and devour the both of them as punishment for love and sin. But the shifting and deep, heavy breathing of her sleeping girl banishes away the spirit of fear, allowing her to close her eyes again, and return to the hopeful tranquility of sleep.

And as if summoned by the audacity of her soul's peaceful dreaming, a voice snaps into her brain somewhere between a dream and sleep...

"You nasty bitch, who the Hell do you think you are?"

And she suddenly feels the rush of icy air upon her naked skin, to pull her from one consciousness to the other, allowing her control of her physical body—raising up in the bed—suddenly wide awake, staring at her short haired, brunette mother, of the Our Lady of the Hips division of latter day motherhood, screaming at her again...

"I said who the *Hell* do you two nasty bitches think you are?"

And Miranda is compelled to tuck her lips in humiliation, brushing her blonde strands behind her ear, face red with embarrassment as she gets out of the bed totally naked, gigantic breasts covered in part by one arm, as she rises to the tone of...

"Take your big breasted, whoring little ass home before I call your mother and tell her what you've done."

And in the wake of this debilitating shame, she gathers her clothes as fast as she can, from her socks to her sweater and coat, slinking a widened, rounded white bottom out of the room.

"Put your clothes on and GO HOME!" are the words she and her lover hear scattered in the air like shards of metal exploded into them, like a sword unsheathed and driven into their guts.

"I was wondering..." comes the muffled voice from behind the locked door. "I was wondering…how long it would take before you showed your true colors. Lickin' and lappin' 'tween a blonde slut's legs…"

"She is *not* a slut— "

"Don't you tell me what she is. I saw it with my own eyes. What were you doin' under there? *Studying?"*

"I love her, Mom."

"You *WHAT?"*

"I said I love her!"

The look of apocalyptic shock on her mother's face is a masterpiece of non-verbal communication.

"So that's why there were never any boys."

"You said that Hell would freeze over before you'd let a boy touch me, remember?"

"And you think that gives you the right to rub crotches with some blue eyed bimbo?"

"Mom stop calling her *names!* She's not a slut and she's not a bimbo!"

From outside the locked door, Miranda can only imagine the profound disgust that twists the mother's features, while she gazes her daughter's nakedness wrapped in a sheet from her breasts to her thighs.

"If you think I'm gonna stand by, and watch you become a cunt licking little whore…"

These words spoken…in the twilight rain. Followed by the mother's step forward in this space, whereby flows the motion of a strong, lovely hand across her daughter's face. And this epic slap brings forth a scream of fear and pain, as the sheet falls halfway down in chaos, as the mother quickly unbuttons her navy blouse.

"You've been begging for this for seventeen years," she says, unzipping her gray skirt, slipping it down and sliding it away.

"Mom, what are you doing?"

And this is answered by another epic slap, which careens the daughter nearly off her feet, as the sheet is pulled so violently away.

"I'm gon' beat it out of ya," comes the backwoods memory vocalized, as the underwear clad woman heavy hands another slap, backhanded into her naked daughter. This one evoking a deeper scream, one with a slant towards that impending onset of womanhood. This deep, woman's scream flies an arrow, invisible through space time, into the heart of the pitiful blonde outside the door.

And the sound of her love being knocked around the room pounds her chest, sending signals to parts of her mind and body, until she is aware of a sudden *iciness* upon the wooden door, and a haze of frost in the air at her lips. And in the haze of this slow motion dream, in a renewed strength of power and self control, she pledges to listen in the calm of uneasy acceptance, and in surrender to the spirits of Predestiny.

She stands there. Her mind alive with images of the unseen. Hearing her friend's scream now muffled by her mother's hand, as the underwear clad woman lays on top of her nude and naked daughter, holding her hand tightly over her daughter's mouth.

"Open 'em up," the mother breathes. "I said *open* 'em," she says. Slamming her big hips down one single time in warning. The daughter raises her legs up in reluctant missionary, to receive a mother's discipline, and the fulfillment of the modern mother daughter dynamic unrestrained.

"You put your face between 'er legs didn't ya?" she breathes, resisting any more than a slow, powerful squeeze of her hips, the flesh dimpling in seemingly every place uncovered by the small, tight underwear. "You put your mouth on her *cunt,*" she says, closing her eyes, her face anguished over by the unseen. "Then you put your thumb in her ass. You put it in there, so she could come *harderrraaaahh….*"

And upon this last, strained and mysterious syllable, she must lower her head, her hand still tight over her daughter's mouth, while the unseen wave twitches the surface of her hips and thighs to alarming strength of motion, in a quivering, shaking that rocks her body from her waist to the fat of her thighs.

In the wake of her body's grieving, she moves to take hold of her daughter's wrists, pinning them to the bed underneath her back.

"If I catch you again," she says, "I'm gon' break 'em."

And this, followed by her daughter's loud, angry scream. A scream burning in the agony of pain, and suffering born of blue and black fire.

The daughter lays there. Mouth open. Eyes glazed in a haze of tears in waiting. Wondering as to the nature of pain, and how the agony of a broken finger could be endured.

Outside the door, the beautiful blonde pulls herself away from the cold. From the cold wood of her lover's bedroom door. In the shock and awe of disbelief, she creeps slowly, quietly down the hall away from the bedroom, opening the living room door in stealth, walking slowly to her mother's car, in the November mist of twilight rain.

Wonder Woman

31

The gray of futures has followed me from Richland Hills all the way to Oklahoma City, to greet me in a swirling of icy Autumn wind and rain. I disembark my windy, silver sky chariot, walking over confidently toward the terminal gate as if I know what I am doing. Trying not to give in to the guilt of this cowardly flight, which saw me run like a scalded dog from the house even before Miranda got home from Emily's where she was supposed to have spent the night. I am sort of glad though, that I wasn't there to deal with the mess she has gotten herself into with Emily and her mother—saying something to me about Emily being physically attacked by her behind a locked door.

"I'm so sorry I couldn't be there. But I thought you were spending the weekend, so I left. I'm really sorry, honey."

"It's okay. If you have to go…"

"It's just an overnight trip, honey. I'll be back before tomorrow night."

"Sure you will."

"Now what's THAT supposed to mean?"

"You know what it means. She's a beautiful, exotic brunette."

"And just what are you implying?"

"That you better behave yourself, Mom."

"Look, I told you, she just wanted me to have dinner with her and her daughter at her house. She wanted you to come too, you know."

"Yeah. I'll bet."

"Look, whatever. Just don't do anything…'dangerous' while I'm gone. Promise?"

"Dangerous? Like what?"

"Oh, I don't know. Something to do with…ICE, maybe?"

"So, what you're trying to say is, 'don't slip on the ice.' Right?"

"Something like that. I love you honey. We'll talk more about Emily when I get back."

"Okay. Love you too."

I had clicked this conversation away, in the aftermath of lying fungalooga—in full blown, false faced pretending that I was not going to see her slam it home to her own daughter right in front of me, after I spill my perverted guts about what I have done to my own.

The pressure of what I have done, the buildup of energy inside is apocalyptic. So much that I was the one who called *her*, to invite myself along on this strange trip to her city.

"I have some things that I have to tell someone. Things that I think you might have a very... special ability to understand. Things I couldn't discuss over the phone, or with anyone else in the world for that matter. Even though my mother—"

And this train of speech was cut off on its own. Met by a silence on the other end that was truly deafening. And this conversation had taken place just this morning, when I was on the way to my cubicle work prison, wishing I'd had the guts to just skip the office all together.

"Buy a one way ticket here for this afternoon," she had said. *"Can you take a half day at work?"*

"I'll use the old doctor's appointment excuse. I can probably be there before six o'clock."

And so, the winds of this strange journey I ride. Having arrived under the gray cloud cover no more than ten minutes ago. I walk confidently with my bags, all three of them (including the two hidden in my gigantic bra under my coat), stepping boldly through the apprehension toward this powerful brunette, toward this Wonder Woman, her arms folded over the front of her burgundy business jacket, leaning back on one long leg exposed in the matching burgundy skirt, her other long leg tilted forward in the perfectly matched high heel, burning a gaze into me as cold and knowing as a hungry white tiger in the snow.

32

The hug we share is laced with profound understanding. So much that I feel as though we know each other better than we actually do. I hug this beautiful woman in the busy airport, embracing her without pretense, following her lead as best I can, until we are a curious pairing for staring. Perhaps, in everybody's mind, she is some beautiful actress or model or TV reporter, hugging her dowdy, dirty blonded, double G-cupped sister.

Without a word, she takes my black carry-on bag from me, and merely tilts a motion of her head, with a knowing smile and twinkle in her eye, walking with as much authority through this busy airport as any passing stewardess who looks upon her with pure envy. And this phenomenon is quite remarkable to see, as one of the overly thin, overly dolled up skinny-pretties walks by, unable to keep from glancing in our direction over and over, until her gaze is locked in the face of my hostess, with a brief look of something close to awe and humility.

And I see this woman of power do this other woman a favor, returning her gaze, coupled with a quick, genuine smile, which breaks the tiny headed, tiny lipped stewardess girl into the biggest smile she has probably managed outside of an airplane in a long time. And part of me is as satisfied as I am intimidated, having watched her win a public woman to woman battle right before my eyes.

We stroll silently through the rest of this latter day crowd of nobody's going nowhere, until we drift out into the cold, Oklahoma gray. The world seems poised on the edge of an apocalyptic rain as we walk, haunting us both with its dreary, oppressive mood. Both of us seem to know that for now, words are hardly necessary, as she reaches back and takes my hand, leading me in a mysterious quiet to black Lexus luxury. She tosses my bag into the back seat, waiting for me to walk around to the passenger side at the end of our delightful quiet game, timing her entry into our luxury ride with mine.

The gray interior surrounds me with endtime desperation, the craving for comfort and emotional security, and the protection from even the echo of poverty and despair. And I notice that upon our soul's deepest sigh, the first drop of Oklahoma rainfall splashes a gloomy warning against our window. And as our view through the windshield is slowly washed away, the two of us sit breathless for a moment, to try and gather our bearings, from having been lifted from the flow of our separate lives, and thrown together in the midst of this cold and tragic autumn rain.

"Did your mother do it to you?"

"Of course she did," she says. Turning to look at me. In the small, closed in space, her enigmatic expression is beautiful.

"And the funny thing is…I don't know if I ever really thought about it until the Grand Canyon trip. Until I met you. That's the first time it happened. I swear to God."

"I don't think you have anything to feel guilty about. The kind of closeness we have with our daughters. Its very special."

"Mother… daughter… *incest*."

In the periphery, I see, I feel the death of pretense. And the burial of cultured civility.

"I call it *love,*" she says. "And I personally don't see anything wrong with it."

"What?"

"I'm not doing anything that a *lot* of mothers and daughters aren't doing in secret. And the thing that really gets me, the thing that really pisses me the *fuck* off, is that they're all chasing down behind their little cheerleader and gymnastic hotties in public, smiling, laughing and hugging everywhere from the football stadium to the church house, and they try to act like they don't have any idea. They try to act so fucking innocent. Well you know what? When I look at 'em, they might as well be made of glass. I can spot 'em a mile away. And if I'm close enough, Hell… I can *smell* 'em."

"You call it love, and yet listen to the resentment in your voice."

"What I *resent*…is the phoniness. The hypocrisy. There's no need for me to tell you the stories of who I know, and what it is they're doing in the shadows. And the fact that you're here… all the way from Virginia, is just confirmation of what I already know. That these so-called heterosexual women? The ones in the suburbs with the absentee, workaholic husbands? The PTA moms and church going mothers, the pastors' *wives* for God's sake—the things they are doing behind closed doors would cause an end of the world *shock* if people knew about it. And the thing is, they can safely hide in the public eye, because nobody in their right mind would believe it, or would even want to believe it. And honey, I hate to break it to you, but I am friends with a female *judge* who..."

"Please don't," I say, holding my hand up, shaking my head 'no.'

"No, you came to me. You called me, and you're gonna hear this. I know what I know about this judge because I *fucked* her daughter... and she fucked mine."

"Oh my *God,"* I say, covering my mouth with both hands in the same shock as if I had seen a little girl run over in a suburban driveway. "So even though you call it 'love,' you're admitting that its twisted. That we are bad mothers for doing it."

"I'm admitting no such thing. I'm saying that some secrets, no matter how beautiful, are better left untold."

"Beautiful? How can forcing your daughter to have sex with another woman be beautiful?"

"Nice try," she says. "Trying to deflect the real issue. Which is that *you* loved your daughter in your own, special way. And because of society's hypocritical bullshit, you feel guilty."

"But... there are rules, aren't there? I mean, what gives us the right to just... make up our own codes of morality? To call everybody else hypocrites because they call what we do sick and twisted?"

"That's very interesting," she says. Gazing into me with a look as sharp as a lady assassin's sword. "You said... what we *do*. Not what we've *done*. You know what that means, don't you? It means that even though you're sitting here with me, close to tears about it, disgusted with yourself about it… you're gonna do it again. And again. And again."

And these words of hers have their desired effect, to run through me with the sword of truth, which causes my eyes to well up from a pain beyond melancholia, where the tear forms on its own, and runs down my face in a slow, steady stream.

33

The house on Heather Valley Road is more typically suburban than I had imagined it would be, being too much a part of the urban sprawl of this Oklahoma City neighborhood; too much money paid for too little space. *Just another glorified suburban doll house*, are the judgmental words of disapproval I cannot stop, as we turn into the driveway and roll up to the garage.

"Home, sweet home," she says. "It's small, I know. But then again, so is the mortgage payment. When I find my mansion, I'm payin' cash for it," she says, smiling a sly grin in my direction, white teeth hidden behind the ruby red lips of legend. Her deep blue eyes are incredibly beautiful.

"So how did somebody as pretty as you become a lawyer?"

"A former beauty queen's got to do something for a living, right?"

"Former beauty queen?"

"I had my run in the pageants," she says. "1ˢᵗ Runner up, Miss Oklahoma USA."

"You're kidding."

"Everybody kept telling me 'you're ready for Miss Universe.' And I was the only one surprised when I made the top five. They all expected me to win. My nickname was *Wonder Woman*, of course. But typical of my luck, they said… '*1ˢᵗ runner up, Miss Alison Brown,*' and they put the crown on some dumb blonde flamingo with giant front teeth and eyes bluer than mine. Even she acted shocked that she beat me."

"Miss Universe… yeah, I can definitely see that. No lie. You have one of the most beautiful faces I've ever seen, actually."

"I don't know about that, but thanks anyway."

"It's true. You do remind me of Wonder Woman."

She laughs a little, unable to deflect the truth from settling in.

"Somebody once said that I didn't look right as a prosecutor. They said I looked like an actress *playing* a prosecutor. So I would wear my hair slicked back with glasses, and that same person said 'honey, you're wasting your time.' I tried only five cases and quit on the fifth case when I lost. I was 2 and 2, and I kind of knew that if I lost, I wasn't meant to be a prosecutor."

"Of course, you weren't. *Look* at you."

"Well," she says, turning to stare at me. "You're not exactly a *hag*, you know. You're beauty pageant material yourself."

"With *this* body? I don't think so."

"You've got the sexiest curves *I've* ever seen. I hope you haven't noticed me staring. People at the airport were staring too. That coat is stuck *way* out there, honey."

"No, it was you they were staring at. I'm invisible."

"Not to me," she says. Not turning her gaze away from my eyes this time. And I notice that though I successfully hide it from her, I feel like an innocent teenager on a date with the school jock, having just pulled into the driveway of his house when his parents are out of town.

"Well," she sighs. "Let's get this over with."

The words cause me to turn a fearful expression towards her, which causes her to laugh a little. In pity.

"I mean this rainy walk to the front door," she says. "What did you *think* I meant?"

"Oh... I, well I just thought... you know. You held my hand a lot on the ride here."

"Oh. You mean like this?"

With her sly, disarming smile in place, she picks up my hand, and caresses it firmly on the back. From somewhere deep inside, there is born the Sapphic intent in me, which will not allow me to pull away.

"My daughter's spending the night with friends, she says. "I hope you don't mind that it's just the two of us."

"I don't mind at all," I say, unable to escape the power of her new gaze, that tells me she is already done with whatever flirty pretense this is.

"Everything about you," she says, moving closer to me, "from the top of your pretty blonde head. To the bottom of your pretty white feet."

And I watch something appear in her features, the power of an instinct born, to where I know that her desire has grown to something akin to hunger.

"And I'm not going to do anything as lame as try to kiss you," she says. "At least... not on the mouth."

This, accompanied by the hint of her smile suppressed, and a return of her caress to the back of my hand, followed by a kiss so perfectly between firm and soft, to where the hunger on her face begins to twist her features to the beauty of anguish, hopeless longing and unrequited desire.

"And I don't want to hear anything about your lovely daughter right now," she says. "Nothing so tired and ridiculous as 'I can't because of her.' I already *know* that. I can feel your hesitation. Your resistance. Your fear."

What magic of Sapphic perception this is, I do not know. But I sit mesmerized by her eyes gazing into me, my lips tight, my eyes widened with the truth she speaks, which is that the types of fear are many. And uniquely distinguished.

34

I brave our rainy walk from black, Lexus luxury to the front door of her two story house, glad that the rain is there in sufficient power enough to distract her from the task at hand. This being to take whatever resistance I have left, and toss it away forever.

The house is dull and quiet inside, devoid of life, as if waiting for whatever reawakening there is to show itself, and to breathe life into it again. Inside, she stops immediately at the bottom of the stairs, touching me on the cheek, brushing the strands of wet hair away.

"You look even sexier this way," she says, taking my coat. Staring at my hair, my lips, my neck... and beyond. "I'm thinking right now that I'm the luckiest woman in the world. I have to confess, I'm a mother lover. There is nothing as sexy as a white hot, suburban soccer Mom. Who hides her beauty in loose sweaters, or loose collar shirts hung down over her jeans. Let me tell you, *Mom...* this burgundy cardigan over this burgundy collar shirt is workin' for you. You think it hides the truth. Maybe from most, who are too stupid or too scared to give a damn. But baby, bodies are my hobby. *Women's bodies,"* she says. Whispering the words onto my lips, causing me to have to close my eyes, and hang my mouth open ever so slightly. But I am forced to open them again, when the kiss I expected, that I wanted, hangs in the balance, somewhere off the shores of my trembling lips and tongue.

"You're scared to death, aren't you?"

"You know I am."

"And don't you know, that apart from money, *fear* is the world's greatest turn on? The world's greatest... aphrodisiac. Stick out your tongue."

This, I do. Sliding it out from in my closed lips in hesitation, as if I were a little girl about to mock her little best friend in somber, serious style.

"Farther," she says. Then upon this, comes her tongue slid out in beauty, where the moisture of it is perfectly gathered, then pushed down upon my tongue in *spit*, which she does not suck or kiss away, but merely backs her tongue away from mine when they touch, undeterred by the line of silken wet and pleasure pulled between them.

Upon the chords of this tragic overture played, she turns me slowly toward the stairs, this ascent toward my demise impending, where the ghost of my loyalty to Miranda waits to be banished out into this cold, Oklahoma rain.

"You know, I've seen great bodies all my life," she says, touching my hips as they switch me up the stairs. But I noticed yours when I first met you, when you were wearing tighter clothes."

"I was 15 pounds slimmer then," I say, very nearly humiliated into a hasty retreat back down the stairs.

"I've seen the so-called definition of great bodies," she says. "All legs and ribs, with two perky foam rubber blobs sticking straight out. But honey, yours is the body... of a sex goddess."

"What?"

"Most women with breasts like yours, they've got no hips to go with it. Or they're overweight with too much hip. But your hips... your *ass*... is extraordinary. And I noticed that not a single inch of that fabulous fifteen pounds went to your waist."

"No. It all went up here and down here," I say, with a humiliated pressing of my hand in both places.

"Oh, yeah," she says. "Top to bottom. From the bottom to the top. Now I see where Miranda got those hips of hers from. The origin of that little goddess frame of hers. Tell me.. what is her cup size?"

"Um... a 36 double G, I think."

She stops us at the top of the stairs, staring at me in the shock of genuine awe.

"And yours?" she says.

"I'm an H cup."

"Hallelujah," she says. Staring down at my loose sweater and collar shirt underneath.

"I was smaller than Miranda before."

"Yes, I remember that. Mother daughter breast queens."

She says it with the fascination of an explorer at the base of a mountain, taking me by the hand and the waist, leading me like the busty, hippy lamb that I am.

To the slaughter.

Jonathan Lovejoy

The Amazon's Curse

35

A hard whack on my backside shatters my pretense like shards of crystalline ice, as I stand in front of the mirror, feeling the burn of it through my long sweater and jeans, amazed at the pissing twinge at my groin. From behind me, this beautiful brunette, hair long and black as the raven's feathers, slips my burgundy cardigan down and away, tossing it unceremoniously to the floor.

"Look at us. Two burgundy variations on the theme. Business casual," she says, slipping her lawyer office jacket away. "And suburban casual."

After running both hands down the sides of my shirt to my waist and hips, she slowly, carefully undoes every button on my shirt, as if to go too fast might cause devastation, to the pleasure of her wait and fervent anticipation. She slides the shirt from my shoulders, down and away from my bra, the awe in her face returning, and I see her reflection in the mirror look away from the gigantic bosom for a moment, staring directly into my eyes from inside the mirror. I watch her in the mirror, unable to take her eyes off my bra's reflection now, while she undoes her pink blouse with determined rapidity, pulling the tight shirt from its tucked in place, leaving her shapely, wide and rounded hips in their burgundy skirt prison.

The tallish business woman in her black lace bra, breasts pushed up in the key of D minor—the sight of her is the dream of every hopeless, dumbbell shaped, pear hipped dowdy such as I, who looks through the catalogues from Pendleton to Penney's in hopeless longing.

"Your body is incredible," I say, my hands suddenly crossed over the front of my humongous bra. "You look like a model."

"Oh, no," she says, shaking her head 'no,' taking both my arms gently by the wrists, lowering them to the sides. "*This,*" she says emphatically, looking back at my reflection again. "This... is a body."

And in the mirror I check her reflection, to see what manner of deception this might be. What trickery, what false flattery as a game she plays. But the anguish on her face is that of hopeless longing realized, to where I fear that if she is not careful, it might well up in her eyes, and flow down her face in a stream of betrayal.

I feel the tremble in her hands at the button of my jeans, undoing the top of them and slipping them down from my hips, her gaze taken briefly by the wideness, the *mom*-ness of my hips at the thighs, to complete my shame, and the sacredness of her discovery.

"Oh my *God,*" she says, sliding the jeans down past my knees, past my feet to the floor. Standing back up straight. Gazing at me in the mirror. "Oh my *Lord,*" she says, unzipping her skirt, pulling it away, kicking it quickly out to the side, then quickly sliding both black stockings off, much to my dismay—having glimpsed the essence of feminine beauty in her just the moment before. But she is determined to bring herself down to earth, down to where I am, so that she can better savor the fulfillment of her heart's desire.

And the start of this, I feel at my backside again, as she *hits* it with all her might, a blow which manages to shake me without lurching me forward, to treat her spirit to the sight of a mighty jiggle, from every inch of me that matters to her. Another whacking of my small waisted, heavy hipped self puts me at the edge of a genuine pain, that threatens to whimper my voice at the edge of reason.

But these whackings were merely in the cause of her fascination with my bosom, my breasts, as she at long last reaches around me from behind, gathering herself close, squeezing both my breasts with all her might—to a corresponding squeeze of her hips to mine, where I feel the knob of her craving and instinct bulged out through her black, silk lace underwear cloth.

And she closes her eyes, engaging this mighty squeeze again, this time accompanied by a trembling sigh in her voice, to betray the extreme nature of what fires have already been lit deep inside. And she knows not to obey her body's call for another squeeze into me, lest she shake prematurely, and cheat herself from the depth of her soul's desire.

She walks with leisure and purpose over to her room sized closet, the light of this Predestiny shining on her athletic, statuesque beauty, showing me every tight, muscled and feminine curve in her body. She steps completely inside the closet, reaching up straight and tall to the shelf high above, to show me the extraordinary roundness and perfection of her hips, a bottom formed so high and tight, to complete the

Amazonian silhouette, which is the power of the masculine channeled through the feminine.

I watch this bubble hipped, bubble breasted beauty take the black, silken cloth down from the shelf, taking from it the form of that which pertaineth to a man, causing me to turn away in the shock of dread, turning back in time to see the beauty slide this long dong up to her groin, pulling at the straps skillfully and quickly, then reaching back to her bra—unlatching it, letting the fabric fall lost somewhere among the infinity of dress cloth and shoes.

Holding it in her hand at the base, at the bottom of the shaft she wields, she turns to switch her woman's hips out into the room, confident in what Sapphira, Goddess of Lesbian Love hath bestowed. She walks slowly, deliberately up to me, pressing her tongue to my lips, in the continuation of what was eluded to before, which is a duet of sloppy wet kisses, where swapping spit is the chosen melody of expression.

She gathers the mouthful of it by desire, to let it fall onto my tongue, where I know and understand that the taste of this spit is fit, to hot wire a hit from my tit to my clit.

And she gathers the spit from my thirsty tongue, to double it in her mouth, and she spits it hard and violent on my tongue a second time, to cause me to gather it up again, and spit it back into her mouth, where the twain of the tip of our tongues do meet, until the streams of it fall from our licking mouths, dripping to the top of my gigantic cleavage below. And I am inspired to lower my head to her darkened nipples erect like torpedoes, to clamp a suck at just a single one of them, gripping her round, tight bottom just in time to feel the first bolt of lightning spark inside, twitching her leg once from top to bottom.

She pulls me up from this vacuum sucking, to return to her place at my tongue, to engage one form of the Nun's Intercourse, to gather the spit again, joining it with what she forms in her mouth this time with noise, *spitting* it hard into my open mouth with violence, and a repressed aggression, pulling tight every hidden muscle in her body.

"I want you on my cock," she says, ushering me to my knees willing, letting the spit fall in a long, glorious glob from her mouth to her member strapped on, which I understand is the road I must take to travel, letting the wet fall from my mouth in grieving upon it, then sliding my lips around her in the Amazon's Curse, which is to push myself down on it, until it is deep enough in my mouth to choke. And this I do again, as she grunts the name of *God* just once like a wild animal, grinding her hips slowly in humping motion, causing me to choke a third time, telling me "don't you swallow that spit, bitch, let it fall on those great big tits— that's right, let me see it fall on those tits…"

And I choke myself a glob to satisfy this goddess, letting it fall over my hands wrapped around her member, to my cleavage spilled out over my bra down below.

As if obeying an order, she grabs my hair with both hands, pulling me up, slapping me firmly but not too hard, slapping me repeatedly enough to sting my face, then holding my head back, ordering me to open my mouth and stick my tongue out, to receive this last and greatest glob of pleasure, gathered in her mouth with a great noise, and spit far back onto my tongue without mercy.

Then, in the wake of this last thrust to my tongue, her lips wrap around it in violence, bobbing up and down the length of it. She guides me closer to the mirror like the abused slut that I have become, so that I can see the teary eyed, heavy breasted whore in the mirror, about to receive the comeuppance that is due, the next comeuppance that is overdue.

And with the power vested in her by the goddess of feminine strength and beauty, she rips my underwear into just enough of a tattering rag, letting the cloth rest low on my hips, the full and bottom heavy hips I see, her fingers fumbling at my backside for a brief eternity, followed by the line of spit fallen in conclusion from her mouth to my rectum, which causes me to tense up in brief worry, as she pushes the impossible into my backside without compromise, sliding it every inch times nine up inside, until I have to cry out as loudly as I can, to let the pain course its way through and out my body.

I take another breath, so that I can sob the next yell into existence, opening my eyes just enough to see her eyes closed, and her face anguished to a beautiful oblivion. She opens her eyes, grabbing the front of my bra at the bottom, raising it up, up, up and away, until the breasts flop down in a phantom chord beyond G Major, flopping heavily against my chest and down near my waist.

"Oh, dear God I've never seen…" she says, leaning me over slightly, staring at the reflection of them that hangs bulbous and low inside the mirror, swinging the sound of what bell tolls for she. "Oh my God I think I'm gonna cum," she says, as though the revelation of it is a fearful thing—gathering one last glimpse of my swinging breasts in the light of sanity, gripping me by the hips, to anchor her body against the trembling that starts in the groan of her voice, as her body begins to shake in sustained energy from the head down to her feet.

She calls the name of God again, as the spirit punishes her audacity, making her have to ram herself into me as though she is possessed, shrieking an angry banshee call out into the air around me.

And in the aftermath of her trauma, I reach back and unlatch my bra, tossing it somewhere far and away, reaching back to the woman who is already spent, moving her hand up to the globes of macromastia, telling her, "clap 'em together, like this…"

And I guide her hands into the perfect rhythm, into the sacred clap of the nuns, into the nun's clap, which she gathers to herself in perfect instinct, holding her lips close to my ears so I can feel her breath, so I can turn to her lips to receive her wet tongue again, as she knows to slam my breasts noisily together without ceasing, until I have to release her tongue kiss so I can breathe, so I can prepare myself for the devastation of my mind and body.

And as I hear a bovine howling from her in my ear, as I feel the tension break in her body again, the energy suppressed in my body suddenly *explodes,* to cause me to feel the power in both breasts unleashed, sent in great, clapping waves toward the center of my body, to meet the devastation at my womb and my bowels, until I understand that I am no longer alive, but have been taken from myself, and thrust in a breathless shaking and grunting somewhere beyond the land of the living.

Full Circle is

Déjà vu

36

Olympian breast fulfillment is the ghost that haunts me, on my return trip from the far city. I had come to my senses on the morning after my epic betrayal, getting up so much earlier than my hostess, spending the morning between the sofa and the kitchen, suddenly struck with an end of the world hunger that cried out for the obligatory bacon in a skillet, which did call her up from her early morning slumber. I endured valiantly her incessant, possessive hugs and morning kisses on the lips and the cheek, the rubs on my back side over the navy blue, silken robe I wore with guilt, successfully hiding from her my desire to run from her in terror, with the intention of never seeing her again. But I noticed that even though I was repulsed by what I had done, I was held by the power of this woman's charm, and the force of her otherworldly strength and beauty.

So, I braved the rest of yesterday, finding it so easy to be phony in her presence, which she dismissed with good natured knowing.

"I know you're disgusted with yourself for what you've done," she said. *"You might even be disgusted by me now. But I swear, I won't pressure you to do anything else you're not comfortable with. To tell you the truth it was... apocalyptic. I've never experienced anything like it. But I don't want you to run. Please say you'll stay with me until tomorrow."*

"I will," I had said. So grateful for the mercy of her perception, which had left me free to breathe, and not feel as though I might suffocate on my own guilt.

In the heart of this brief memory of yesterday, I languish at our walk through the gigantic Oklahoma City Mall, where I am so proud to be seen in her presence, wandering from one end of the retail prison to the other. She never misses an opportunity to point out candidates for her latter day lust, showing me the pleasures of some shapely young blonde or whoever; girls out in front of stores doing some pointless thing or another with signs and displays and balloons for children, some of these girls with shapes as impossibly compelling as can be.

One light skinned, young black beauty's hips are just too much for her to pass up, and she wanders the busy walkway, to where this yellow skinned beauty is biding her time as a perfume store princess, bugging passersby with unwanted sprits and sprays of perfume, prattling on about specials and sales inside the store.

"Joleen," is the name she gives my lawyer friend, who stands there looking the girl up and down her tight t-shirted, tight faded blue jeaned body, giving her one of her beautiful beige business cards with the raised brown lettering, coaxing the girl's phone number onto the back of another.

"When I come back I'm bringing my daughter to meet you... she's about your age. I'm having a little mother-daughter get together at my house soon, and I'd love for you and your mother to come. I'll be sure to give you a call."

"Okay, I'll be waiting to hear from you. It sounds like fun."

"You better believe it honey," Alison says. Smiling that wry, disarming grin of hers, mouth closed, eyes twinkling. Hugging the big boned beauty with a quick, side peck on the cheek. Backing away, looking the girl up and down again, waving goodbye as I do the same.

"That's the difference between you and me," she says. Glancing back at the seventeen year old, golden skinned beauty. "I don't hide the fact that I want to fuck her."

"And so, you're saying that I'm a hypocrite. Because I don't hit on every pretty girl that I see."

"Not *every* pretty girl," she says, smiling at two young skinny pretties walking by. "Just the ones you want to fuck."

As we stroll further away, I glance back at the light skinned black girl with the big hips, having to admit that I do understand what she means.

"Tell me," she says. "What do you want to do to her? Don't think about it. Just tell me."

But truthfully, I do have to think about it.

But not for long.

"I want her butt naked on the floor. Maybe, sweaty after exercising in the living room. Her, not me. I'm in my bra and my underwear. She's naked, her hands underneath her between her legs. This big butt of hers raised up just enough. And I just want to straddle that big, yellow ass of hers, and grind that thing until I get *all* the way off. Until I have to shake from top to bottom."

"Oh my," she says. Staring at me in gleeful astonishment. "You *nasty* bitch."

I tuck my lips, lowering my head in mock shame, suppressing something close to a sinister laugh.

"Don't tell me that at long last, I have found a true partner in this crime."

"I don't think so," I say. "Not that I'm too good for it or anything. But the truth is... I have my daughter to consider."

"How so?"

"My conscience. What I did with you is the first, and the last time."

She glances at me again, as if trying to understand what manner of new creature this is that has suddenly appeared beside her.

"I knew it was too good to be true," she said. "Somebody smart and beautiful like you, but down to earth and real. I was kinda hoping..."

"What?"

She braves the barrier of this question. Letting the pause flow through this space in time.

"Why am I like this?" she says.

"Like what?"

"Why do I have this craving inside? This burning that won't die? You were just a witness to it. If it takes me a year, I will have that girl underneath me. Screaming her head off for me to please stop fucking her. And I don't understand why."

"Were you hoping that I would be there to help you do this? To help you find pretty girls to be with?"

"Actually," she says, ushering me to the nearest bench for us to sit, nearby a blonde, shapely teenager, helping young toddlers onto a tiny merry go round. "Actually, I was hoping that you could rescue me from it."

We both watch the perfect, pretty teenage girl with the long, silver blonde hair, foreshadowing her suburban, show wife future.

"I was 22 years old the first time I did it," she says. "I was a senior in undergraduate school. I answered a job post looking for a part time, live in nanny for law students. I knew I was going to get the job even before I showed up. I've always been lucky getting jobs. What I had with her wasn't an interview as much as it was a private begging for me to let her hire me. And the strange thing is, that a part of me resented this woman for having the... the *balls* to hire somebody else to take care of her daughter. Even though that somebody else was me. Instead of just staying with her husband and being a good mother, and doing it herself...

"I mean, who does this uppity bitch think she is, to pay me like some peon, to kiss her and her daughter's ass for nine dollars an hour plus room and board. I mean, you could tell by the house that she was rich as Hell, even though she only ran a little hole in the wall flower shop. Something her husband's money kept going. I think she was just glad to have the privilege of a nanny. And she *loved* the fact that I did beauty pageants and was planning to go to law school. She was too round faced and matronly for my taste, this woman. But she had the most beautiful little twelve year old girl. This little brunette, shapely little woman in a girl's body...

"The little girl was so happy and outgoing, and she would actually whisper in my ear sometimes with both hands cupped over my ear... *"My friend's Mom dances naked in front of the mirror,"* she said. And of course, my instincts went off like a fire alarm. Instincts I didn't really even know I had, Alison. And the first thing that came out of my mouth *was "My Mom did something even more wild than that."* And this little girl said *"What did she do?"* And I said, *"I'll have to show you, but it's our little forever secret. Promise?"* To make a long story short, we were both naked on the couch. I was on my back. And I had her hop up and down on me until my vision hazed, if you will."

She looks over at me, in time to see me put my hand over my mouth. Staring deep into the theater of my mind, at what it shows me of the twenty two year old beauty, and how the spirit came to the little 12 year old that day.

"And when I *came,* the girl had the presence of mind, the natural instinct to lower her head and suck my breast. I'll never forget what her hopping up and down on me did to my body. I'll never forget it. And then when she attached to my breast..."

I listen mournfully. As her voice takes on a somber, faraway tone.

"When my daughter was a little girl, I was terrified to leave her alone with my mother. Because somehow, I knew that she couldn't wait, to do the same thing to my daughter, that she did to me."

The face of despair fades into my brief memory, as I watch my soaring chariot's descent through the clouds, returning me to the gray, rainy world below. I survive this brief eternity on the runway, rolling hopelessly through this cold, end of the world rainfall. Full circle is déjà vu, drawing me down the current of predestiny toward the gate, where I am in grieving for a return to my own private insanity, and to escape the tentacles of the beautiful Alison Browne conundrum.

As I wonder what evil spirit moved to send me to Oklahoma City in the first place, my heart leaps from a spark bestowed by a vision. This, the sight of my daughter standing at the end of the tunnel, like a light inside a dark dream.

Waiting for me.

37

We allow ourselves the biggest, bustiest hug this airport has seen in a number of years, I'll bet, to give every so-called reunion a run for its money, with my arms raised high as I step against her body, hugging her around the neck while she hugs me tight around my waist. And neither do we hold back with the kissing pose, to make those around us wonder what manner of sickness this is, and whether or not we can possibly be mother and daughter. *They're not sisters, to be sure. Friends neither,* they say. *But how can an aunt and niece, how can her daughter's friend, how can her mother's friend hug and kiss her on the mouth like that? The kiss was held too long,* they say. *The hug was too relaxed and deeply committed,* they say. *They act like they are in love,* they say. *So how can they be mother and daughter, with such an inappropriate kiss in public?*

My daughter takes my bag happily from me, putting her arm around me as we stroll through the busy Richmond airport.

"Feels like you were gone for a week," she says. "I missed you every second."

"Really?"

"Of course I did. I hope you're not going back there again."

"I hadn't planned on it."

The people all swarm and hurry around us as we walk, all so heavily focused on wherever it is they think they need to go. None of them understanding what messages are told in the latter day rains, and of what warnings await them in the swirling autumn wind.

"There's a little bit of a surprise waiting for you in the car. I thought I'd warn you."

"*Warn*? Oh no... please tell me you didn't by that stupid dog we saw..."

"No," she says, shaking her head. "But that dog wasn't stupid. He was adorable."

"Yeah, in the pet store he was adorable. I'm just glad you didn't buy it. Or that cat either for that matter. I don't know whether people know it or not but cats are bad luck on four legs."

"They are not," she says, giggling again. "It's nothing like that, I promise."

"Well, what is it honey? I'm not in the mood."

"You'll see."

Ice

We take the last steps from the busy desperation, drifting through the big sliding doors, underneath the outside shelter. To my utter disappointment, I notice that our silver SUV is nowhere in sight. My daughter unfurls her tiny black umbrella, holding me close beside her, refusing to walk us any faster as we step out into the grieving weather, walking tall and strong beside me, like the mistress of the Autumn rain she is.

These rains fall with a new and steady assurance, as though the grieving earth has been infused with anger, where the prevailing mood is one of impending devastation and misery. But even as the Winds of Eschatology swirl and blow against our brief wilderness walk, somehow I feel safe and protected in this autumn rain, and comforted by the ice maiden walking beside me. The words "you didn't forget where we parked, did you," push at the tip of my tongue in a fury to get out, as I hold my mouth shut tight, waiting to see what surprise it is my daughter hath wrought for her mother.

The big parking lot is alive with splashing drops of this November rainfall all around us to infinity, to drown every sense of hope for a reprieve—as I finally see the silver Pathfinder in the far off distance, seeming so lonely and isolated from the other cars scattered about. Hardly in the mood for a single word about our sojourn—our infinite walk from the airport to our ride—I take the last few steps under our Autumn umbrella, so glad to finally be getting inside our familiar space, inside our rolling silver chariot, so appropriately named for our tragic search through the rest of this miserable life.

My daughter closes me up on the passenger side, tossing my bag unceremoniously in the back, allowing me to breathe a cold sigh of relief in the daytime dark, as she walks slowly, enigmatically, around the front of the car...

And in the periphery, as if conjured from the substance of a nightmare, I am suddenly aware of a slow moving figure dressed in black, raising up from in the back seat like the spirit of Death, causing me to turn my head on the speed of pure instinct, and shriek the pain of what icy claw has gripped my heart and squeezed it, long enough for it to skip a beat or two...

With my hand over my mouth, I gaze into the eyes of melancholy that stare. Eyes of a pale skinned, lovely brunette ghost, who gazes at me in tuck lipped humility, touched by this selfsame spirit of ice, cold, and fear.

"Surprise," she says. Timidly.

In the daytime dark, her voice is low.

Almost whispery.

$\mathcal{O}$ur rainy trip home is a threeway filled with tension. Neither of us being able to push through the veil of cultured civility beyond Emily's plight, which shows me images of the girl being beaten by her mother.

We drive on through the gray cold, feeling the early departure of autumn this year, and the early arrival of winter's angry touch in our hearts and minds. And I notice that while my daughter drives us home through this icy November mist of rain, I feel a craving toward her reborn in my physical body, born from roots that run deep, tapping the recesses of both my soul and spirit.

The beauty of mother daughter sex permeates my soul to infinity, as we finally find our way to this side of our rolling trip through this wilderness. We all valiantly brave our way through what tension there is that remains, disembarking our rolling chariot into the pre-winter rain and wind. The three of us move quickly through the oppressive November cold, settling into the tranquility of our working class suburban home. Whether or not the burning I feel for her is mutual is no concern of mine, while we settle our guest down into Miranda's room for the rest of the day and night, where we know Miranda's 50-inch Samsung will be the noisy cure for what ails her.

"I need to steal your friend away for a few minutes honey," I say. "Make yourself at home. Don't worry about dinner, we're doing take out," I say on the way out, though food is the last thing on my mind as I walk with my daughter hand in hand down the hall to my room.

And no sooner than the door to my bedroom is closed and locked, that our lips are locked as well, in a deep kiss heavy with reunion, and the reminder to us of who we are. This kiss is reluctantly released, long enough for her to breathe... "But *Emily's* here, Mom..."

I can only answer, "I know," and "I can't help it," licking a kiss to her long and beautiful neck that I must restrain, lest I bruise a hickey as a give away to my perverted secret.

The spirit of reluctance suddenly creeps into my daughter, where her emotional loyalties are divided just enough, to add sweetness to this tart elixir, to water my mouth with a desire unfathomable.

My hands move on their own, rolling her pullover shirt up over her bra, then raising it up, grabbing the fabric and going forward with a mighty pull, flopping the two big globes down against her body, the sight of which sends a warm tingle to the center of mine. And this warming tingle down below grips hold of me and spreads dangerously, as I take hold of both of them, pulling one of her nipples hungrily into my mouth.

"Please," she whispers. "Oh, *please,* Mom. I feels too good. I'll make too much noise," she says, which has the final effect on my body's response, as the sucking ignites an explosion I cannot hide, which twitches my leg so violently that I nearly lose my balance, but holding onto the suck, fighting against it like an Amazon on the battlefield, unable to suppress the powerful grunt and heavy breathing through my nose. And this happens though I am fully clothed, with neither a button nor zipper undone, feeling as through a spirit tossed a grenade from my soul down into my groin and my womb.

The valiant effort to suppress this orgasm nearly makes me dizzy, making my daughter rub the side of my head, then run her fingers through my hair in support. *Stay on her breasts*, my instincts whisper to me, which I do gladly, knowing that this selfsame, merciless spirit from the timeline has moved into her, and is about to drop a bomb inside her as well.

Bob your head to one nipple, I hear, which I do with deep commitment and enthusiasm, as if I were starving and the flavor was strawberry. Upon this pale brown nippled, strawberry delight I give suck, until my daughter warns me," Mom I'm gonna *scream,"* and I reach up and cover her mouth completely, shocked by the noisy power of the muffled scream against my hand.

It would have been a siren for the ages, probably heard by our guest anyway, but neither of us able to care one iota or another. I raise up from this breast fulfillment, from this breast devastation, bringing this latest trip full circle, locking my lips again to hers in a breathless kiss, where we are unable to hold it for long, until I have to release it and hold onto her tight so that I can breathe again.

And in keeping with what I know of my daughter's need, she turns her mother around, lowering both my jeans and hers, reaching under my shirt to my bra. From behind me, with both our underwear cloths intact, she grips my gargantuans over my bra, then pulls them both out one at a time, holding onto them still under my shirt, then begins to slam herself noisly into the back of me, where the clapping of flesh is the tell-tale sign to what or whomever may be listening, that an end of the world tension has to be built up, and then broken to cause annihilation in the body.

And this, my daughter begins to achieve, her movements born upon a rhythm involuntary, hard enough to jar my insides from top to bottom, as her youthful libido takes hold of her senses, strengthening her body, causing me to have the good sense to hold my head back toward her just far enough for her to find my tongue with her lips, so that her gruff, low pitched animal grunting is channeled discreetly down into my body. This noisy, bellowing sound betrays the wildness of this second rise and fall in her spirit, which I feel in the tight grip of her hands at my breasts, and the convulsive shaking of her entire body against me.

But in the aftermath of this trauma, is the birth of another rise in tension that must be broken, this one inside her mother's body. I turn to her, hugging, kissing her face and neck gently, then pulling her shirt off over her head, then bending over to slide her jeans away. With my own jeans pulled up and still open, I usher this huge breasted girl over to the bed, her underwear cloth still in place, breasts hanging from underneath her bra, laying her down spent onto her back on the bed. The feeling inside me is as deep hunger unsatisfied, causing me to lay on top of her, lowering my pants again, leaving my underwear over the widened hips, pulling my shirt up to expose the giant globes, letting them mash and collide down against hers, to draw of their own accord the rhythm in my hips, as I begin to repay my daughter's indignity—humping, bumping this grind *hard* between her legs opened wide, not knowing how I am able to feel such a profound connection in this grind, but knowing only that I cannot, that I must not stop this Waltz of the Tribades, where I can feel her nipple so blessedly poking against one of my own.

Of this impending loss of sanity, I have no control, laying full on top of her, my shirt up and pants down, my daughter in her underwear, in awe of what possibilities through forbidden pleasures may come. *Put your tongue in her mouth,* is the warning instinct that forms, which I do in the nick of time, as the spirit tosses another grenade from my soul, exploding my body into a chain reaction, that rises from my hips up into my breasts, holding me at the fearful edge of the unimaginable, until this explosion obliterates the new tension in my body, groaning the gruff, hopeless scream into my daughter's mouth, as the cataclysm quivers my body in waves from head to toe.

39

*I*n the aftermath of our deep perversion, I leave my daughter and her guest alone in the house, long enough to fly to one of the steak food places, something called The Outback, whose popularity hath bred contempt among the uninformed. This apocalyptic hunger we all feel must be dealt with at long last, where the protein of medium rare New York Strips and Baby Back Ribs will aid the cause of our continued survival.

"It's too good to be true," Emily says. Sitting on the edge of the bed in Miranda's room. They sit with the lights completely out, save the glow of light drifting in from the hall. Outside, in the twilight, the shimmering earth lights illuminate the rainfall against their early evening window.

"What's too good to be true?"

"Your mother," Emily says. "And the relationship you have with her. Does she know about that power you have? That end of the world thing that you can do?"

"Of course she does. I told you that, remember?"

"But... but what did she *say?*"

"She said she wants me to feel normal. She doesn't want me to retreat from society, to become a recluse."

"But how long do you think that's gonna last? It's a part of who you are. It's a natural instinct. You can't suppress something like that forever."

Outside their window, the Autumn wind swirls the rain against the house.

"What would you do if somebody made you mad? I mean... can you even imagine something like that?"

"No."

"Well, if I had what you had, based on what I saw, I would freeze my mother's head into a block of ice, then I would take a baseball bat and *break* it into a million pieces..."

In their early evening dark, Emily swings her phantom bat upon the proper syllable.

"That's gross, Emily."

"Well, so is my Mom. You heard what she was doing to me, didn't you?"

As Emily watches her friend lower her head, too embarrassed to speak of it, a flash of lightning glows quietly from the November clouds.

"I guess it's true what they say?"

"What?"

"There really is no thunder in a November rain."

Emily continues to gaze at her beautiful and voluptuous host, marveling in the soft light the depth of her physical beauty.

"You know what?" Emily says. "You're prettier than she is."

Miranda speaks only with a deep, questioning stare.

"Samantha," she says. "It makes her helpless against you. She can't successfully turn anybody against you because of it. Everybody's always liked you. I think that's why they're so angry. Because you chose me over them."

"But what exactly does that mean, Emily? *Chose* you over them?"

"Don't do that sweetie," Emily says, shaking her head in absolute resistance. "Don't play that naïve pretty girl with pretty smile. Who pretends she doesn't understand why the other girls don't matter."

As the lightning glows outside the window, Miranda slides over to her best friend, her soulmate, her lover. Putting her arm around her gently. Resting Emily's head against her bosom.

"Please don't let them hurt me," she says.

"I won't. I swear to God I won't."

A harsh gust of wind gathers the rain unto itself, splashing it against the window and the outside walls with the fervor of a cold storm in July.

"I'll let you in on a little secret, " she says. "The thing that you and your Mom have. The power I heard coming from the bedroom earlier today…"

Yes. Indeed, the types fear are many. And uniquely distinguished.

"I think it's beautiful."

The Nature of Fear

"Residents of Richland Hills, Virginia are stunned today from a claim made by the principal of prestigious Amber West High School. The forty nine year old female principal was apparently abducted and raped by four unarmed assailants. The abduction was captured on school security cameras, where four masked figures dressed entirely in black are seen struggling with the principal at her car, pushing her into the back seat, then driving away. The principal says she was driven to a wooded area north of town, where she was held prisoner and raped by one of her abductors. The four figures remain unidentified, and police have no leads, although the principal claims that at least one of the four attackers was female. Other than the video footage of the masked assailants, the investigation has turned up no further evidence at this time. Cora Leeds, the Associated Press."

$\mathcal{T}$he school is alive with these apocalyptic rumblings, that of their sexy and sophisticated principal, and her recent journey through Hell on Earth. *Ms Greer got raped*, is the somber and bizarre refrain spread around, like the proverbial pebble in a pond, and what happens to the surface when it is tossed in. From the center of this latter day happening, throughout the whole of Richland Hills, on past Richmond, over the Atlantic coastline and west over the Blue Ridge Mountains, the truth about end of the world humanity spreads like a prairie fire in summer heat, that there is no stopping the flow of time and history, and that the impending end of the age is here. *Her breasts were bitten*, is the rumor flown around the school in delight, as the rest of the world joins in the apocalyptic discovery of the third part of the truth, that yes, the one who raped the female principal was a woman.

And this revelation begins in slow earnest, to gradually freeze the hearts and sensibilities of those who choose to deny it, that endtime woman is wayward, and the uncovering of this is the last and greatest sign before The Rapture and The Second Coming. This, when maybe a billion souls will be changed in the twinkling of an eye, and be lifted away from this great and beautiful blue hell we live in, on the eve of mankind's final departure. These are those things which are written, as human behavior begins to prophecy—that these are the last days, and that this is the twilight of humanity.

The teachers, students, the office staff and the new lady principal— a dowdier and more matronly version of the same, but disarmingly kind hearted and reserved—all of them mill around the school about the day's business, a few days before the Thanksgiving break, in the heart of this Autumn rainy season. These souls are adrift in the cloud of this latter day happening, in the unbearable cloud of rumor, and the fog of unbearable tension and fear.

And through this fog of melancholy and gray, the doors from the outside are pulled open, and into the busy morning crowd arrives the first of the Four Horsemen, which are the Death, Hell, Famine and Pestilence of cultured civility. In walks four of the prettiest, sexiest teenagers in the world, stopping in ultimate power and confidence among the lesser beings who stroll and drift around them in daily apprehension. Four adult girls who found one another, who crossed paths that merged here, at this condemned and unfortunate place in time.

Ice

Samantha Daley, Kelly LeMonde, Rosalyn Reynolds and Jennifer Lynn Johnson. Newly adrift in this morning crowd, this morning cloud of rumor, as the four of them spot all at once their future prey, standing nearby her locker with a load of books in both arms folded in front, staring back at them in a broken, fearful expression. And much to her cold and fearful dismay, Samantha stops the four of them like a white engine train, then turns to walk back to where the brunette stands in nervous awe. Waiting.

"My, my. If it isn't Witch Hazel. And her dyke friend."

This, she says without even as much as a turn of the head, to look at the brunette's blonde companion in the eye.

"Doesn't Witch Hazel look pretty today," she says. Touching Emily's hair. "Your hair's not as greasy as it usually is."

Kelly turns her head away, closing her eyes, tucking her lips to suppress a powerful laugh.

"When my hair gets wet," Samantha says, sniffing a lock of her blonde hair, "mmm... sweet. Smells like straw. When your hair gets wet," she says, gently twisting Emily's hair onto her finger, "it smells like a pet store."

The laugh that Kelly had worked so hard to hold in scrapes its way out in the loudest snicker in God's creation, causing Emily to glance fearfully at her.

"Awww, but what difference does that make," Samantha says. "Half the time, you stink anyway."

"That's *enough*, Samantha," Miranda says, grabbing Samantha's wrist, pushing her hand away.

"Oh my God," Samantha exclaims, laughing delightedly. "Why are your hands so *cold*? You freak."

"It's because she's scared to death, that's why," Rosalyn says.

"Her hands are so fucking cold it's scary. Like a refrigerator."

"Or a morgue," Kelly adds. With a sly, devious stare.

"Yes, that's it," Samantha says, looking at Emily through an expression of false pity. "A morgue."

"I said leave her alone."

"Oh yeah?" Samantha asks. Stepping directly in front of Miranda. "And exactly what are you gonna do about it, bitch?"

The two blondes rest still on the rhetorical, with secrets, threats, and all manner of answers spoken in blue eyes that stare.

"You're on thin ice as it is, baby. I would suggest… that you keep your mouth shut."

"Or else," says Rosalyn. Blazing a fiery look at her.

"Or else *what?*"

Rosalyn's satisfaction at Miranda's naiveté breaks her concentration, enough to cause her to turn away from Miranda's pathetic bravery.

"Any time you feel squirly baby," Samantha warns her, "you just jump. Because I know how bad you want me. I can feel it. You just let me know when. And it's you and me behind closed doors. And one thing about it is guaranteed, honey…"

Emily stares intently, her entire spirit clung tight to Samantha's dark promise impending.

"…I am going to break your fucking arm."

And in the wake of this tragedy spoken, Samantha allows all of the comic delight to drain from her expression, where a sober, fight night stare is revealed.

"Samantha, please," Emily says. "We're both really sorry for what happened."

"Sorry? Sorry," says Samantha, the delight returning to her mature, womanly features. "Let me be classic for a minute," she says, smiling at the brunette, "and say… no, you're not sorry. Yet. But you're going to be."

The two victims glance at the four merciless expressions. Gauging within themselves the nature of fear.

"Oh, that's a shame what happened to principal Greer, isn't it? She was such a nice lady. She cared so much about all us girls. She wanted us all to succeed. Be a *strong* woman, like her."

Emily notices Jennifer Lynn's delighted, determined stare, as Samantha leans in toward her, touching her lips to Emily's ear. To whisper the third part of the truth. Which is cataclysm.

The shock freezes awe into Emily's features, as they watch the four girls return to their track, gliding back toward wherever it is in the gray world they are going to.

"What did she say?"

From the mournful, defeated gaze, Emily blinks away the emotion welled up in her eyes, which rolls down her face in a slow, steady stream.

"It was them."

Jonathan Lovejoy

Kelly LeMonde Rides the Wind

elly LeMonde rides the wind. On the eve of eschatology.

A failed, frustrated beauty queen. Busty, brown haired, brown eyed beauty for the ages. The vicarious channel through which her shorter, less beautiful, more voluptuous mother has lived. Having won and lost every beauty pageant and contest imaginable, from the age of seven to seventeen. Trophies, ribbons and tiaras too numerous to count. Memories of secret disciplines too numerous to bear.

Kelly LeMonde rides the wind. On the eve of eschatology.

A competitor in the state finals for Miss Teen Virginia USA. The pinnacle of her mother's hopes and dreams. The penultimate goal on this part of the journey. A goal unrealized in this competition year.

In the heart of memory, Kelly rides home humiliated with her mother. Having not even made the top fifteen in the pageant. Left standing on the stage in the forest grove of other trees. Trees left unchosen and forgotten. Standing there. Smiling, clapping for the fifteen finalists. Never daring to look out over the sea of desperate onlookers. The mothers and sisters of desperation. Craving so intimately to see their daughter, their sister do the impossible. To win this lottery to become queen.

In the heart of memory, Kelly rides home from this last and greatest defeat. Having to gauge the nature of fear. The physical and emotional pain it causes. Sitting in this evil waiting. Waiting for her mother to cease the cold shoulder. Waiting for her to speak.

"You lost because you're too fucking FAT," the mother finally says. Greek blood burning in the summer night. In the heat of these failed aspirations. Of her daughter's perceived disobedience and betrayal. *"I told you your tits and your ass where too big...why the FUCK didn't you just stop eating?"*

Upon this vulgar syllable, comes the mother's hand onto the daughter's mouth. Flashing a ball of lightning to her brain as they drive. The daughter holds her mouth open so that she can breathe. To try and medicate the rising emotion. To try and block its climb into her heart. Into her eyes. But this, to no avail, as the world around her suddenly begins to shimmer. But a shimmering that draws her eyes to blink on their own.

"Oh you may as well save that honey. Cause I swear to GOD you're gonna need it. Because when I get through with you won't be able to wear a bikini for a MONTH."

Kelly LeMonde rides onward. Defeated by her mother's silence. Choked by the unbreatheable tension in the air. Wondering of what possibilities lie in a mother's dark promise, and whether or not they can truly be fulfilled.

The Cadillac SUV rolls into the driveway of the southern brick palace. Dr. LeMonde's small fortune, mortgaged to eternity. Good credit. Good salary. Good life.

Eva LeMonde and her daughter disembark their rolling Cadillac luxury. The wide hipped, round breasted woman waiting. Grabbing her daughter by the arm. Digging her thumb painfully into her bicep as they walk. This young beauty queen, a head taller than her mother, being pulled along in a secret prelude. A precursor. A preamble to suffering.

Upon the crossing of the threshold. As the earth turns toward the evening.

"Get your FAT ass upstairs and take off every stitch of your clothes."

Wiping her eye, sniffing, the daughter goes toward the stairs in uncertainty. Not knowing whether her soul is more of a prisoner of grief or fear.

She takes the steps in the weight of worry. Taking each heavy, nightmarish step toward the den of secrets. Toward the golden oakwood luxury of her mother's upper room.

In her mother's bedroom, Kelly stands in front of the mirror. Gazing the beauty of a somber expression. Undoing each button in defeat. Knowing that her parents are too rich. Their house too luxurious. Her mother too pretty and sensual. Her homelife too privileged for her to run. Her life with her mother too comfortable for her to flee. Because of her mother, she is a teenage beauty queen. A goddess among ordinary girls.

Kelly LeMonde rides the wind. On the eve of eschatology.

Watching her white skin appear slowly in the mirror. Her shoulders, arms and waist. Hips and her thighs. And then her breasts in the key of D Major. Hips fattened to fertility. Body parts stubbornly inherited from the heavy hipped, heavy breasted Eva. The short haired, short legged Lady of the Hips. A body unfit for the beauty stage of her youth. Hips too wide at the thigh. Haunches too ripe for the picking. Hips handed down to the next generation. The companion of a bosom too heavy to ignore. Bodies curved for the ages, the two of them.

For the daughter, huge lunches at school and off campus. Heavy early dinners away from her mother's sight. To kill the hunger just enough, to put on the pretense at dinnertime. To please her mother.

The mother comes into the room. Still fuming from her daughter's big time loss. Fully clothed. Long sleeved navy blouse, navy blue skirt in place. On high heel pumps of repressed rage, she steps lively over to her daughter. The smell of the fermented grape in her breathing.

"Put your hands behind your back," the mother says. Taking hold of both the daughter's nipples. Turning. Twisting. Pulling. Pinching. Turning them again as a faucet to elicit the flow of sound. The flow of a scream. *"This is why you lost,"* she says. *"Because you disobeyed me and ate like a fucking pig before the biggest pageant of your failed, miserable LIFE."*

Upon this syllable comes the twisting. The chiming of another scream. Another scream into the upper room.

"I TOLD you, you were too heavy, didn't I? DIDN'T I! You had the biggest tits and the biggest ASS on whole goddamned stage. You looked like a fucking PIG!"

And upon this last and greatest syllable, twists another burning for the ages. To cause a shaking of the daughter's head. A slobbering. A pleading for mercy.

The mother releases them in a hard, biting pull. Stepping away quickly to the closet, to retrieve the black leather in waiting. She returns to her weeping daughter, her arms crossed over her burning breasts. The mother takes firm hold of the folded serpentine, the black leather belt in classic whipping form, grabbing her heavy breasted, heavy hipped daughter by the arm, wildly strapping her across her buttocks and the backs of her thighs. Using the power of her easy command, dominating the girl in a mother's Amazonian strength unleashed.

"Hold still... I said HOLD STILL!"

And this, the daughter does. As the mother refocuses her strength and skill, bringing the rest of the many scores of blows across her daughter's naked buttocks. Lashing herself to exhaustion. Whipping her daughter's white skin to blood.

"And if you think it's over," she says, breathing heavily, *"think again."*

In the mirror, the daughter sees her mother's reflection move away, back to the closet. And to her dismay, the mother stays inside for too long, shuffling and fumbling about, until she emerges in the nude, her widened hips in epic contrast to that which pertaineth to a man—the thin, red line, the bright red rod of correction raised and ready for battle.

The daughter can only open her mouth in ghostly form. Her face the embodiment of tragedy, as the mother steps over to her beautiful daughter in front of the mirror. Placing one hand around the girl's throat, fumbling at her backside, spitting onto her finger just enough, touching it to the red line member. Pushing it into her daughter's rectum without mercy. Feeling her daughter's body in Olympian resistance defeated, as the daughter shrieks in wicked banshee form; a yell of pure anger and pain uncovered.

"I told you," the mother whispers heavily, *"if you lost again, I'd make you regret it for the rest of your life..."*

And this, upon a single, massive slam into her daughter from behind, causing her to shriek again, her face twisted into the ugliest cry that her beauty can manage. And in the wake of this, the mother stands perfectly still, her face suddenly awash with worry and fearful expectation, moving her hand away from her daughter's throat, barely able to control her own deep, heavy breathing.

And as though powered on their own, her hands grab hold of both her daughter's breasts as if for dear life, as she stands perfectly still, as if moving would be disastrous to both her body and soul. But this inevitability is as the turning of a day, as the energy rises at both her nipples against her daughter's back, until they strike a lightning spark to her groin, causing her to grunt a deep, gruff *"Oh...GOD"* for the ages, as her body takes over from her mind, and slams her repeatedly into the back of her daughter, as the wave of energy grips hold of every part of her, erupting from her voice in a battle cry from east of Eden.

She slams this violence into the back of her daughter without mercy, until she is finally able to stop, feeling the remainder of the wave pass through her hips, quivering them once in a mighty shaking, then quivering them mightily once again.

The daughter stands there. In the aftermath of her mother's trauma. Gazing the face of regret. A body and soul of defeat.

Kelly LeMonde rides the wind. On the eve of eschatology.

In the Light of

Woman to Woman

*I*t was *them?*

This is the question that haunts my mind. Words that I spoke to my daughter just last night, when she spoke this end of the world impossibility to me. Words that my daughter's new soulmate had gathered unto herself, when Samantha Daley had whispered a tragic vulgarity in her ear yesterday morning…

"When we fucked that uppity bitch," Samantha had whispered, *"she came so hard she pissed herself…"*

Ice

And I had warned my daughter with a mother's instinct for protection; *"Don't go ANYWHERE near this."* Sometimes, it is truly better to let sleeping dogs lie, so to speak, and absolutely *no* good can possibly come from their involvement. Even if they did it, there is absolutely no proof, no evidence that they could have ever been involved. And the inherent brilliance of the girls' act is that no one in their right minds could ever believe it could happen.

These four horsemen of the apocalypse haunt the theater of my mind, when the chimes to my old flip phone interrupt my lonely strawberry desert in front of the TV. Reluctantly, I leave both my deserts behind— that of glazed strawberries and Cool Whip, and woman to woman violence impending—answering the phonecall from somewhere in the great beyond.

"Hello?"

"Hello, Cynthia?"

"Yes. Whose speaking?"

"This is Alison. Alison Browne."

And against my will, by an instinct beyond my control, my mind fills my body with cold regret.

"Alison, hello. It's great to hear from you."

"I'm... I'm sorry to call you like this. I... I just missed you."

"I missed you too. That was some first date we had, wasn't it?"

"Oh...yeah. Truth is, I was...I was wanting us to get together again. I'd pay for your ticket of course. This time we might do a little traveling. Spend some real time together."

Walls and barriers do rise and fall. To usher us through the maze of this life. To make inevitable every choice that is meant to be. Every word spoken. The depth of every breath we breathe.

"Alison, I wish I could. I really do. But my daughter needs me."

"Well... the way you had to see me before, because you had something you had to discuss. I'm sort of going through the same thing. It's about my daughter and me."

"What is it?"

"I can't discuss it over the phone. I really need to see you."

"I understand. But now is not a good time, honey. The drama in my daughter's life is so thick, I couldn't leave if I wanted to."

"I understand. Do you think maybe I could come and see you?"

Barriers do rise and fall. From here, to the end of this present age we're in.

"It's not a good time, honey. I wish it were, but like I said. I have to think about my daughter."

And suddenly, there is the requisite, dangerous pause. Like car lights flashed off on a dark country road.

"Were you thinking about your daughter when you fucked her?"

"What?"

"You heard me, Cynthia. You left her just fine when the guilt from it was eating you alive and you had to come see me. And now that you're over it, you're over me too, huh?"

"Alison, don't do this. Please."

"Don't do what, baby? Call you out on your bullshit? You and your daughter are best friends now, so you suddenly can't stand the sight of me? Is that what I was to you? Just some filthy fuck in another city?"

"Alison, what's wrong? This isn't like you. You're stronger than this."

"There's no need to patronize me to satisfy your guilty conscious. I knew you were disgusted with me when you left. Oh, my God... I've actually been humped and dumped."

"No you *haven't.* I told you, I..."

"Just save it, Cynthia. If you still cared about me we wouldn't even be discussing this. I'd be on my way to your house tonight."

In this new silence, there is the clamor of tragedy. Of truth.

"Okay then. You and your daughter have a great life."

"Alison..."

In the wake of this final word spoken. In the light of woman to woman violence promised and fulfilled. I flip this tragic phonecall away, suddenly unmoved by my strawberry glaze desert uneaten, or the two beautiful, suburban women locked in such violent conflict on the television screen.

Across the rainsoaked prairie of Oklahoma. Over the rainy streets and suburbs of the far city. The winds of eschatology swirl and blow a cold warning through the modern mother daughter dynamic, touching those mothers and daughters who they will, to cause the death of cultured civility among them.

These winds roam the streets of Oklahoma City. To find where Alison and Laura Browne believe they have hidden themselves from the tragedy of loss, and from the cold hand of hopelessness and despair.

Alison stands at the window of doom. At the back patio door, facing the heart of this latter day rain. Feeling at last the grip of what she has spent a lifetime running away from, a lifetime of avoidance and denial. In the heart of her briefest memory, she recalls from this self same hour, when the third part of the truth gave her its icy touch in this cold, Autumn rain.

"Mom, I just don't want to do it anymore. Okay?"

"Do what? You mean us? What we have?"

"Everything, alright? I can't believe you tried to use me to pick up that girl in the mall."

"I just wanted you to meet her. Was there anything wrong with that?"

"No, you wanted me to *recruit* her. To add her to your little collection of girls and their moms you have *sex* with."

"Laura, where is this coming from all of a sudden?" Alison says, grabbing her daughter's arm, spinning her around firmly. "I thought we had an understanding."

"I don't wanna understand it anymore," her daughter says. Emptying her dresser drawers into the big, black suitcase one by one.

"Just come here a minute, baby," Alison says, her grip transformed to a firm, but gentle coaxing. She leans in to her brunette daughter's lips, only to have the kiss blocked by a turn of the head, and a massive pulling away.

"Honey, what's wrong? Why are you doing this?"

"Because *this* is wrong, Mom. I don't want to do that anymore. It's just too weird, I can't *stand* it anymore."

"But you don't have to leave, Laura. If you don't want us to do that anymore we won't. Just please stay, honey."

"How can I stay here? Knowing what you are? What you do behind closed doors?"

"Don't try to act so innocent Laura. You told me that you kissed Beth Hall's mother at your last sleepover."

"I didn't kiss her. She kissed *me* in the kitchen. And it was just a kiss."

"A *deep* kiss, you said. You said it lasted at least half a minute."

"Mom, that was like a year ago. I've changed since then. I don't like it anymore."

"Its him, isn't it?"

"Who?"

"That damned *boy* you've been seeing. You *never* would have acted like this if it wasn't for him. If I had known dating a boy would have turned you against me I would have never let you do it."

"Why? Because you want me to become a closet dyke like you?"

As if under its own energy, Alison's hand raises, moving through their small space with force and power. Slapping her daughter hard enough to turn her head, and flash a bolt of lightning to her brain.

"This, from somebody who has fucked half the cheerleading squad. I am still your mother you insolent little... and I will *not* have you stand here and suddenly judge and disrespect me because you sucked a boy's cock and you liked it."

"And so what if I *did*," she says, tears streaming down her face. "Not every girl and their mother is a *lesbian,* Mom."

"You're right," Alison says, her features stern with a mother's frustration. "Just the mothers and daughters that *we* know."

Laura can only lower her head in her own frustrated defeat, unable to recollect a single one of her pretty friends who has not engaged in the unspeakable.

"And your running away from me to live with your father isn't going to change what you are. And you can choke on as many boy's cocks as you want, Laura. But trust me, it won't change who you are any more than running away from me will. I have watched you do things with older women honey that would make a porn star jealous. You wield that strap on like a *weapon,* baby. Your dyke blood is thicker than mine."

"Yeah? Well if it is, who made it that way? Who says I even wanted to be like this? I want a different life, Mom. A better life. I'm tired of being a lesbian *slut* for you and your friends."

The brunette beauty returns to the task at hand. Slipping the rest of her folded shirts into her suitcase. Moving down to the next drawer, the ones with the many different colors of turtle necks she has hardly ever worn.

"Laura *please*," her mother says, touching her daughter's face gently. "Please don't leave me. I'm so sorry."

"It's too late, Mom. I can't stay here anymore. Knowing who you are. And what you do. I just can't be a part of it anymore."

"But we don't have to do that anymore. I swear we don't. Just please. Please have mercy."

"I'm sorry," Laura says, staring her mother in the eye. "I can't."

In the same battlefield shock that every dying Amazon feels when they are run through, Alison allows for the calm of uneasy acceptance, her mouth slightly open in brief amazement, turning, walking slowly out of her daughter's room. She goes to the golden oakwood nightstand, sliding the bottom drawer open. From the same shoebox of legend that every bottom nightstand drawer has hidden at one time or another, she pulls out the black, semi automatic pistol. Then, strolls as casually as a day in the life, back down the upstairs hall to her daughter's room.

When she steps inside, every wall in the house bears witness to the sound of a daughter's screams. To the words formed, "no… please Mom, *no!*" Followed by the noisy blast of gunpowder, and a chasm of silence in the aftermath.

In the wake of this tragic memory. Somewhere in the heart of the far city. Alison Browne stands at the back patio door. Gazing out into the storm. Wondering where it is that her beloved daughter could have gone.

As the pain gathers itself in a mist at her grieving eye, she blinks this melancholia down her face in the requisite slow, steady stream. Raising the pistol to her mouth, wrapping her beautiful lips around the barrel.

The house resounds with another quick, thunderous blast of noise, as the beautiful woman falls crumpled and lifeless to the floor.

The Modern Mother Daughter Dynamic

"*olice in Oklahoma City are investigating the apparent murder*
suicide of a successful real estate attorney and her daughter in the
affluent Brittany Oaks community. This is the first killing ever recorded
in this wealthy suburban neighborhood, leaving residents there stunned
over the incident, many of them well acquainted with both the victims.
The seventeen year old cheerleader and member of the National Honor
Society from Oklahoma City High School was found dead in her bedroom
from a gunshot wound to the head, and her mother was found in the
kitchen, with what investigators are calling a self inflicted wound from

the same gun. Those who knew the former Miss Oklahoma USA Runner up claimed that she and her daughter were extremely close, and were friendly, outgoing members of their suburban community. Family and close friends of the mother and daughter are the most baffled, claiming that they showed no signs of conflict with one another, and that the two of them quote 'had never been happier.' Cora Leeds, the Associated Press."

he death of Alison Browne reminds the world of the modern mother daughter dynamic uncovered, which is filled with violence and perversions unseen. And every so often, the current of truth that runs beneath swirls an eddy at the surface, so that the public is called forth from naiveté and complacency. These are the last generations of motherhood, and the last generation is imminent, here at the twilight of humanity.

And I am a hidden purveyor of this dark truth, this undercurrent of mother daughter perversion, so that the truth of Alison Browne fills me with every other emotion than guilt, relief and regret not being the least among them. Part of me is greatly relieved that I was nowhere near her and her daughter when this insanity broke. And part of me is deeply regretful that I ever knew them. And I am even touched by an echo of anger at her, for calling me on the eve of her tragic breakdown, to agitate my nerves with her own emotional turmoil, then try and torment me forever with guilt from beyond the grave.

But in keeping with the twisted side of who I have become, the death of Alison Browne and her daughter serves to fill me only with *lust*—and a sudden, fierce sense of possession and craving for my daughter, where my entire body is tense with desire.

"You know what Emily said," Miranda whispers to me, squeezing my breasts from behind, "she said what we had was beautiful. She asked me could she please watch us do it next time."

"This is between us, baby," I say, standing in front of her in my underwear bottoms, leaned over while she stands tight against me from behind, leaned over my back, massaging both my breasts with a slow, smooth and steady squeezing, letting them fall, swinging down low and heavy, running her hand back and forth across both nipples, the feel of which reminds me of a match against the side of a matchbox, being slid repeatedly over it unsuccessfully, but knowing that its fatal flash of light is impending.

Into this breast play, I have coaxed my daughter, having spent the entire day thinking of nothing else—from when I heard the radio voice drone her deep, power woman tone about the mother daughter suicide, through every long, dreary hour at my office computer typing, through our time spent with her and her new friend at the big mall in Richmond, to this brief time at the eleven o'clock hour, when my daughter literally snuck out of her room when she believed her friend was sleeping.

Somewhere on the near side of the midnight hour, I lean forward in the fullness of this desire, my daughter behind me in full contact, her bra and underwear still in place, with my bra long gone, and my underwear bottoms slid down low on my hips, my hands nowhere near the improper place inside them.

With both hands gripped at her thighs behind me, I lean over in full concentration, but focused on just how little I have to concentrate at all while she does this, as she continues to run her hand across both my nipples without ceasing. And I notice that deep within my groin, in my womb, I feel the rise of an energy undeniable, risen higher up with each new stroke across my nipples, anguishing my face in shock and awe, taking control of my breathing away, until this feeling inside suddenly joins the energy risen in my breasts, until it seems that my entire body is a flame burning inside, to where I know that soon, this wave of energy will crash, and nearly devastate me from head to toe.

And at the moment of my most profound disbelief, at what pleasures the human body may manifest, the feeling in my womb erupts violently, and I feel my legs and hips quiver into a full shaking that I cannot control, causing my daughter to use her strength in full to hold me, allowing this earth quaking to escape loudly in a battle cry born of its own volition, as though brought forth by a spirit of repressed rage unleashed.

And then, the remaining tension breaks all at once, making me glad that I am already doubled over and held tightly in her arms, as she still strokes my breasts across the nipples without ceasing. Every brushing across them brings a deep grunting from my voice, and another spasm of shaking that I find impossible to control. This, my daughter does without mercy, until every quiver of this wave has passed into oblivion, and I am leaning up against her, with her massaging both my breasts heavily, lowering me from the heights of trauma, down to the depths of love and tranquility.

Jonathan Lovejoy

Rosalyn Reynolds Rides the Wind

*R*osalyn Reynolds rides the wind. On the eve of eschatology.

A family of female fighters, they are. With nary a trophy or ribbon among them. Not a single class. Not a single formal competition. Already a private history of violence. A single mother and three daughters. Rosalyn and her two sisters. Backyard and bedroom brawls along the timeline. Hardly a week in their lives passed without some combination of physical conflict between them.

Rosalyn Reynolds rides the wind. On the eve of eschatology.

A mother forcing her daughters to fight one another since they were small. Making the girls fight to exhaustion behind closed doors. *If you've got a problem, fight it out*, she always said. *And the loser is gonna have to deal with me.* Losing fights with her older sister since she was eleven years old. Beaten up by her repeatedly through time. Taking her first beating from her fourteen year old sister back then. Through the years as her sister got older, through the older sister's eighteenth year and beyond. Enduring brutal belt whippings from her mother when she loses.

You two are gonna strip naked and fight or I swear to God I'm gonna beat the Hell out of both of you. I swear to GOD...

A 21 year old sister, still living in their working class home. Unable to achieve her own space in life. A minimum wage job in a local warehouse assembly. Not knowing why she would rather live in a twenty years war with her mother and sisters, than go out and live on her own.

Eighteen year old Rosalyn rides the wind. These, the winds of rage and fear. In the mother's bedroom of their little home, stripped bare of their clothing. Breasts wobbling, hips jiggling free. Both young women bent over in a mutual headlock, having been told already, *and the looser is gonna get the BLOOD striped out of 'em this time. You two bitches don't want to get along, then fight it out...*

The eighteen year old junior struggles mightily against her angry, failed older sister. Punching her in the face. Getting it harder in return. Both sisters refusing to give an inch, until the older sister's strength prevails, and she flips the eighteen year old to the bedroom floor. Falling down on top of her. Punching her hard in the cheek, the ribs, her stomach, her breast.

Oh, yeah... you got it GOOD this time, the mother says. *This is a good one...*

Rosalyn flips away from her older sister's hold. Trying to hold her down. Trying to wrap her legs around her. Grabbing her hard by the neck with her arm.

In the small bedroom space. Slamming against every painful side and corner of furniture wood. The older sister manages to twist out of her younger sister's grip. Flipping over on top of the naked eighteen year old. Undeterred by the punching. The pushing and clawing at her face. Laying hard on top of the naked eighteen year old. The mother noticing the tell tale twitching of her older daughter's buttocks. A twitching by involuntary means. A twitch of violent victory.

In the aftermath of trauma unseen. In the wake of a lightning bolt passed through. The older sister straddles the eighteen year old girl. Punching her hard in the face. Drawing the requisite red flow from her nose. Lying her body in full over her chest and her face. Locking her down on her back.

Rosalyn Reynolds rides the wind. Kicking. Pushing. Twisting. Writhing her body. Until the muffled defeat calls forth, *I can't breathe...I give you fucking bitch. You stink, get the fuck off of me!*

In the delighted pain of this insult, the older sister moves up past her sister's shoulders. Straddling her crotch into her face. Unable to notice her mother's removal of her own top and her bra.

I'm NOT gonna lick your pussy you nasty bitch!

Do you give up?

I said YES!

Say it again...

I GIVE!

The older sister rolls off of the eighteen year old. Her face alive with the power of sadism. The delight in causing pain.

The mother takes every stitch of her own clothing away. Breasts hung low in the key of D minor. Hips exaggerated in mature femininity. Legs thick and strong from the farm of her youth.

The mother orders the eighteen year old to the dresser. Standing her up firm and strong, leaning her forward on it with her hands. Raising the leather belt of legend. From her daughter's buttocks down to the backs of her thighs. Every new welt is created on top of one before. Striping her daughter's white skin to blood.

Christie, bring me that strap on, she says. Watching her younger daughter's pained reaction. Feeling the pleasure of it in her own body.

The mother straps the full sized phallus to her hips. Placing the head of it to her daughter's rectum. Pushing it painfully inside, to the melody of her daughter's pitiful screaming.

Momma please... it HURTS! she says. This, serving only to cause the dark blonde woman to push and pull, in and out, until the white phallus is covered in blood. Pushing it in and out until it is fully lubricated in red. Drawing energy from her daughter's scream. Telling her older daughter *put your hands over her mouth.* This, spoken in the nick of time, as the word *mouth* is the last sound she can make in full sanity. Bellowing like a branded bull in her daughter's ear. Eyes rolling back. Body alive with shaking, quaking energy.

Rosalyn Reynolds rides the wind. In the pain of predestiny come and gone. In the burning of blue and black fire.

Rosalyn Reynolds rides the wind. On the eve of eschatology.

Jonathan Lovejoy

Purple Melancholy

"re you and Emily lovers?"

After my body's first trauma has come and gone. We lay calmly in each other's arms, in the bed of my twisted affection.

"Yes. Is that okay?"

"Truth is, I was hoping you weren't."

Outside the nighttime window, these darkened rains fall in perpetual grief and warning.

"But I understand it. I do. She's your soulmate."

"You're my soulmate, Mom."

"I'm your sick, twisted mother," I say, tickled by the truth and tragedy of it.

"I'm just as sick and twisted as you are. I can't even imagine us not being together anymore."

"In my heart, I judged Alison Browne and her daughter. When I'm doing the exact same thing as them."

"How many other mothers and daughters are like us, I wonder," she says.

"I don't know. But I'll bet its more than people can possibly imagine. I mean, look at me, for God's sake. No one would... no one *could* even suspect me."

"Alison did."

"But the interesting thing is, I had never, ever imagined that I would do something like this. What we do, Miranda, I can't even say it out loud in here."

"I fuck my mother," she says. Raising up slightly, leaning her face over mine.

"I... I *fuck*... my daughter."

This grips the two of us as though it were a revelation. Sparking a flash of energy passed between us, as she lowers her lips to mine. Gently. Touching this kiss from top to bottom, from the bottom to the top, stopping just long enough to say softly, "I want you to *fuck* me, Mom."

In her voice, there is such a desperate, crying need from somewhere along the timeline, from somewhere through the generations passed down, to whisper those powerful words through her unbeknownst, to activate a mother's deep, possessive love inside. I push my kiss heavily to her lips, pushing my tongue deep into her mouth, rolling over on top of my beautiful daughter, finding her proper place down below with mine, as she raises her legs far back in classic missionary, as I can only slam myself into her as hard as I can, one single time, as if no other motion is possible—repeating this, staring her in the icy blue of her eyes, almost completely hidden from me in the dark.

The look of painful anguish, I can barely see; the desperation I feel in her calls to me, twinging me at both my nipples through my breasts, to caress my groin as though in pissing promise, raising my hips up again, bringing them down, to listen to my daughter's lovely whimpering, and to feel the craving of her soul's need to move.

But I must abandon her need, for my own selfish whim—to satisfy a craving deeper than hunger, beginning to slide my groin against hers after each heavy slamming down, until the feeling causes my vision in the dark to haze purple melancholy, and the sound I hear flowing from my mouth is the deep, tragic grunting from ages long gone.

"*Y*ou did *what?*"

In the shock of genuine disbelief, Rosalyn stares at her lovely blonde mistress, who sits at the weight machine, opposite the gym wall mirror, her arms raised and holding onto pulling levers. Every pull inward towards her chest flexes the tight, powerful muscles beneath the firm, feminine form.

"So what," she says. "What is she gonna do?"

"That bitch is a tattletale, Samantha. She already got you suspended over that stupid witch note, remember?"

"You think it's not still bothering me every day? Just last night I dreamt the bitch pushed that same note in my face at school. When I woke up this morning, I already knew what I was gonna do."

"What?"

The strong, shapely blonde relaxes the weight machine from one last pulling, stopping to gaze at the feminine strength and beauty in the mirror. What other women and men there are milling hopelessly about have faded to insignificance in her sight.

"I think you already know what," she says, standing up from her open legged view of her reflection. In unspoken awe, her friend watches the blonde cheerleader and Judo champion wander over to the leg curling machine, laying face down on the cushioned bench, her purple sports bra bulging mightily from the pressing. The wide, rounded buttocks are packed tight in matching purple sheen.

"When I was in church with my mom on Sunday," she says, her legs positioned to raise the curling bar, "a Bible verse came to me that I had heard of, but had never read."

In the leg curling machine, as she lays face down on the cushioned bench rest, her leg muscles flex the limits of their calling.

"Was the preacher preaching about it or something?"

"Hell no," she says, exhaling, straightening her lower legs again. "All he ever talks about is money and happiness. As if God actually gave a damn about either one. No... this verse just sort of slid into my brain. And I don't think I've actually read it before. I googled it when I got home. I found it in a place called *blueletterbible.org*. You know what? I think the Bible might be the best book ever written."

"Since when did you start caring so much about the Bible?"

"I don't," she says. "I'm just telling the truth. It's some good shit in there, believe me. I had to stop reading it because it started to scare me."

"That's because you're evil."

"And you know what? So are you and everybody else. Especially in church. I've been hit on by four different married men before."

"What, in church?"

"That place is a fucking *joke*. It's like going to some glorified Christian concert every Sunday. Everybody in there is gonna burn in Hell and they know it."

Rosalyn is unable to avert her gaze from the wide, rounded hips of her mistress, flexed to big bottomed glory in the melancholy purple stretch tights.

"Anyway," she says, "this Bible website had the whole chapter this verse was in. Trust me, the Bible is *amazing*. I might actually read it someday."

"What was the verse?"

"Oh yeah. It was the book of Exodus. Chapter 22. Verse 18."

She lowers her legs to straight again. Staring at the big cleavaged, blonde, ponytailed stranger in the wall mirror.

"Thou shalt not suffer... a witch to live."

The rains of Autumn sweep in cold rage across the Virginia countryside, swept up from the Atlantic coast in anger and grieving, past the beaches abandoned in hopelessness for another cold and perilous journey on this part of the ecliptic plane, as the earth prepares to die again for another season.

Miranda and Emily find their way through the unrelenting autumn gray, through the mist of weeping blown in from Melancholy Bay, back to the empty park of faded autumn green. Emily sits in mild bewilderment under the shelter. Sitting on the picnic table, with her feet resting on the bench, watching her friend, her mysterious lover walk so strangely, so casually out into the rain. She looks on in awe and nervous apprehension, wondering what cold insanity this is, and whether or not this is the moment she realizes that her gifted friend has no trick beyond a frozen tree limb or two, and this is where they both will realize that the poor girl is a freak that has lost her mind.

And in the rainsoaked fog of this worry, her fears are confirmed by the sight of her silver blonde, wet headed friend in black boots and matching rain cloak, holding her arms out to the side in the shape of a cross. *Oh my god, she's crazy*, are the tragic words that form in Emily's mind, in her spirit of fear, as she suddenly sees the bottom of her friend's cloak begin to flutter wildly, along with the locks of bright golden hair in stark contrast to the midnight fabric.

There are no tall grasses around the center of this madness, the center of this chaos she sees, to illustrate the power of what appears to be the rain gathered up and *swirling,* moving in a circular pattern that grows wider by the moment, until it is clear that yes, this is a wind and it is moving *fast,* growing outward—outward from the figure dressed in black, until Emily suddenly feels droplets of rain attack her in a bitter, biting swarm, and a powerful whooshing of the *iciest* breeze she has ever felt, and a feeling that if it goes on, she will be gathered up in it, and tossed into the storm like a wayward leaf blowing in the wind.

And in her periphery, in the corner of her eye, in the mist of the gale force wind as cold as ice, she sees the edges of the woods bend and sway violently, accompanied by a single flash of bright lightning from the sky to somewhere beyond the trees, and a blast of thunder from the twilight of human history. The 'oh my God' of worry is transformed in her heart to one of pure terror, as she holds on to the table laid down, hair blowing as wildly as the treetops tall, until the wind dies down as suddenly as it began, allowing her to see her breath appear in fog, and feel the touch of pure arctic *winter* on her skin.

With an ice cold hand, Emily brushes the hair from her eyes and sits up again, gazing across the open park space at the figure dressed in black, who suddenly stands with her arms down, her black cloak framed in the picturesque drifting of a sea of flakes in white, crystalline form.

Jennifer Lynn

Johnson

Rides the Wind

51

*J*ennifer Lynn Johnson rides the wind. On the eve of eschatology.

Catholic. Oldest of seven children, five of them of the sisterhood. A mother widowed since her oldest daughter was twelve, when the father died of pancreatic cancer. Leaving behind a wife and seven children. A woman who had allowed her Catholic husband to penetrate her only once a month. A woman who had ruled her husband with this diversion.

Jennifer Lynn Johnson rides the wind. On the eve of eschatology.

A girl introduced to her mother's perversion, less than a month after her father's funeral. The oldest of the five daughters, the two sons notwithstanding.

I want us to do something together that is so secret that we can't tell another living soul the rest of our lives, because people won't understand. It's just between us, okay? Do you want to do this secret with Mommy?

The twelve year old girl nods her head in wide eyed, tuck lipped form. Leaving her eyes wide open when her thirty seven year old mother presses her lips to hers. Coaxing the little girl's lips untucked. Pressing her big lips to the little girl's eyes. Gently closing them one by one with a kiss. With the bedroom door locked and bolted. With her other six children at play.

The mother removes her twelve year old daughter's dress, t shirt and underwear. Standing the little girl up in front of her. Pressing her tongue in an ice cream lick to her daughter's puffy, pubescent nipples. Sucking one deep into her mouth with the audacity of a slurp. With quiet sucking, suction and popping noises unrestrained. Knowing she cannot suck her daughter's half developed breast again, lest the burning in her own groin erupt into an inferno. A flame colored in royal blue tinted black.

The mother stands up in front of her daughter. Undoing every button of repression. Every button of suppression unbridled. Removing her shirt and bra. Exposing a woman's bosom, a key played in high, rounded C Major form. Coaxing an erect nipple into her daughter's mouth. Standing firm in her long, loose flower made skirt down to her ankles.

Pull on it real hard, the mother says. Nearly loosing herself again to the lightning stored in her body. Finally having to remove the long, poverty mother skirt, shoes and socks. Exposing the big, snow white cotton underwear, stretched far across hips too large for her frame. A set of haunches never meant to be seen. Hips widened at the thigh in mammoth girth. To deliver one of the most classically feminine shapes on earth. Hips kept hidden in modesty over the years. Hidden by repression.

The mother slides her underwear down from her big, shapely bottom. To reveal in full the creative power of God. The echo of Eve past down. A waist hardly curved, fit and straight, offset by the width of the female form in jubilee.

I want you to get behind Mommy, she says. *I want you to grab Mommy's bottom with both hands, and I want you to jiggle it real hard...*

The repressed, Catholic mother stands there. Understanding already that her husband's touch was dead in comparison. The feel of the girlish hands—clawing, squeezing, shaking her buttocks—rises the ire in her groin again. To give her warning of what must be done.

Spit on your thumb, she says. *And stick it in Mommy's bottom...*

This, the little girl does. Lips tucked in concentration. With nary an understanding of what must be.

With only an unfathomable pressure of undiluted feeling. Pushing a pissing twinge to her groin, causing her to grab hold of one of her own nipples for support, eyes closed, mouth open of its own volition. Suddenly feeling the blast wave begin at ground zero, somewhere beyond her groin, somewhere beyond her rectum, spreading out into her entire lower body, causing her buttocks to shake uncontrollably. In the girl's delicate hands, as she keeps her thumb inside her mother, listening to the energy wave flow out of her mother's voice in a low, pitiful moan of quivering helplessness and defeat. The mother tenses her bottom mightily, squeezing it around the girl's thumb pressed up inside, unable to stop a second and equally powerful wave of energy, shaking her buttocks in a mighty wave of quivering again, with the same deep, ghostly moan in trembling from somewhere deep inside her body.

In the aftermath of this trauma. The mother stands in breathless surrender. Giving heed to every seducing spirit. Understanding when a private life's calling has been answered.

Jennifer Lynn Johnson stands up behind her mother. Wrapping her arms around her in revelation. Inherent knowledge of good and evil born. Kissing her mother on the back. Comforting her. Marveling at the strong twitches still present.

The mother ushers the girl to the bed. Sitting at the edge of it. Taking a stocking from the nightstand. Tying it around her own ankles. Sliding up onto the bed. Laying down on her stomach. Coaxing the girl to climb on top of her, and lay on her back face down. Her little groin at her mother's big buttocks. Telling the girl, *slide your hand between Mommy's legs. Rub inside where you feel Mommy's thing. Where you feel Mommy's girl cock. It's called a girl cock, baby. Say it for Mommy...*

Girlcock, the girl says. Hardly a whisper of understanding truly wrought. Barely an echo of this deep knowledge born. *Rub your hands against it,"* her mother says. *Now slam your thing hard onto my bottom...*

This, the girl does. Slamming her little groin into her mother's big bottom with all her might. Noticing with each slam, her own feeling growing inside. Realizing that she is unable to stop herself. Unable to stop this steady 4/4 time. Rubbing her mother's place below. Hearing the mighty, quivering groan in her voice again. Wondering if she can stop herself from shrieking from the cataclysm in her young body.

Jennifer Lynn Johnson rides the wind. Forward along the timeline, to the present autumn day. In the cozy hotel with her mother. Protected from the icy rains of November. Protected from listening, prying eyes that stare.

The seventeen year old girl slams her full, rounded bottom onto her mother's widened hips. Caught up in the rhythm of the day. A rhythm born from when she was twelve.

Jennifer Lynn Johnson rides the wind. Her hands below, at her mother's proper place. The improper place. Slamming this rhythm, to the melody of her mother's long, ghostly moan.

Jennifer Lynn Johnson rides the wind. On the eve of eschatology.

Fire and Ice

"Oh, what are you two a *couple* now? I think I'm gonna be sick."

Samantha and the other three horsemen take their places around Emily and Miranda's cafeteria table. Outside the window wall, the rains of this November's grief fall without ceasing.

"Samantha go to Hell," Emily says.

"Not before you, baby. Which is where you're gonna be soon if you don't watch your fucking mouth."

"I'm not afraid of you anymore, Samantha. So you can say whatever the Hell you want."

"You being afraid of me isn't the point, Witch."

"Oh, really? Then what is?"

"It's you being taught a lesson."

"What are you gonna do? Corner me in the girl's locker room and beat me up after school? How pathetic is that?"

"I'll show you how fucking *pathetic* it is," Samantha says, sending Emily's open milk carton flying against the glass wall. The streams flowing down the glass trickle in winter white.

"Samantha let's go," Jennifer says, taking hold of Samantha's arm. While still leaning over the table towards Emily, Samantha turns her head slowly to burn a gaze into the eyes of betrayal.

"What?"

"You can't afford to get in anymore trouble. You'll be suspended longer next time."

"So what is this, a threesome now? You're gonna try to get sandwiched in between 'em?"

"It's nothing like that, Samantha. I told you I don't want any more trouble."

"Well, *I* do," she says, turning back to stare Emily in the eye. "I want my hands around her throat so bad I can *taste* it."

As if activated by this last, aggressive syllable spoken, Miranda reaches across the table towards Samantha's wrist.

"Miranda, don't," Emily says, shaking her head no.

"That's right, Miranda. Don't."

But in their look is exchanged a spark of warning. A flash of angry resistance from the blue eyed ice queen.

"You know what," Samantha says. "I've had just about enough of you looking at me like you want to do something. I said... stop *looking* at me."

Miranda glances over at her friend across the table, at the fearful pleading look in her eyes. Then reluctantly, accompanied by a deep, frustrated sigh, Miranda looks down at the table.

"You just saved yourself a bloody nose, Icy. And I've got three witnesses here that would swear I was just defending myself against you when you grabbed my wrist."

"And pulled your hair," Kelly chimes in smoothly, glancing first at her blonde mistress. Then, at her blonde, blue eyed victim.

"Yeah," Samantha says, smiling a wry, closed mouth grin. "And pulled my hair."

In the periphery, Samantha's tough, pretty girl enforcer Rosalyn laughs a little, arms crossed, lifting her thumb to her tough, pretty girl mouth. Biting her thumbnail. Staring delightedly at the two girls having this waking nightmare.

"I don't know which is weirder," Samantha says, standing up straight. "A November snow… or a clit licking witch."

Jennifer Lynn turns away, shifting her body slightly, her features twisted by a judging, disapproving sigh.

"Oh, what's the matter Jenny," Samantha says. "Are you mad because they won't let you play Cunny Honey with them?"

"Oh, my *God,"* the beautiful Kelly says, mouth wide open, staring in total shock and glee at Samantha.

"That's right," her mistress says. "Lickety split."

In the midst of a cruel burst of laughter, Samantha, Kelly and Rosalyn turn to leave, stopped short when Samantha turns suddenly, stepping back over to the table.

"I almost forgot. You two lezzies have got the whole school talking already. Hottest couple this school has ever seen, they say. Fire... and *Ice.*"

Samantha turns away again, tickling the air with "clit to clit," descending herself and two of the girls into another chorus of brutal laughter.

"Meet me in the library after lunch," Jennifer says softly, gripping Emily firmly by the shoulder. "I need to talk to you."

"Jennifer, come *on,*" Samantha says sharply, turning to glare at her like an angry mother at a busy twelve year old. Jennifer hurries away obediently, joining the laughing trio on their way out of the school cafeteria, half of the students staring at the walking drama in total bewilderment, and the other half in tragic understanding. The two girls glance at the busy room full of nosy onlookers, noticing that every corner of the cafeteria contains a brutal stare or two.

Miranda boldly watches her brunette friend, as she turns away from the quickly maddening crowd, gazing at the streams of milk still visible on the glass—as the cold, unforgiving rain falls in a gray mist outside their window.

53

"You can't trust her," Miranda insists. "She is best friends with Samantha *Daley.*"

"And that's why I *have* to trust her. You saw how she was in the cafeteria. You and Jenny Lynn used to be friends, you said. I can tell she's not as bad as those other three."

"Emily, you can't even trust that she's gonna show up here. She said 'meet me in the library after lunch.' Well, where is she?"

"She'll be here. Just give her a few more minutes."

"We're skipping class because of this."

"Who cares? This is more important than some stupid math class that makes me want to drop out of school anyway. Every single day. I *hate* that class."

"I hate going to class too, but still. We have to go. What the heck does she want to talk to you for anyway?"

"I'm praying that she'll help me," Emily says. "Samantha Daley is dangerous, Miranda. Even *you* couldn't stop her without doing something... something we can't talk about. And I thought I was over it until she got in our faces again today. Miranda I'm still scared to death. I have such a bad feeling..."

"Look... you don't have to be afraid of them anymore. As long as we're together, we'll be okay. Besides, nothing's really going to happen anyway. She's just trying to scare you. And I don't believe for a second what she told you about... about that..."

As an echo of a recent memory, she sees Emily look fearfully into the nearby distance, watching the Fourth Horseman of the Apocalypse turn the corner from between the shelves, and drift toward her.

"Hi, Emily. Miranda. Miranda, is it okay if I talk to Emily alone?"

"Where are your friends?" Miranda says. Boldly.

"They're in class. They don't know anything about this yet."

"Yet? About what?"

"It's alright, Miranda," Emily says.

"Are you sure? I can stay if you want."

"You better go on to class. I'll be alright."

Miranda stands up, bold and strong, a head taller than Jennifer Lynn. Between them is a tension for the ages. Energy built up from as far back as the eighth grade, when a girl named Samantha Daley first came between them.

"I just want to talk, Miranda," she says. Voice trembled under the weight unsettled. "You can't protect her. And *I* can."

Miranda's eyes are suddenly as relaxed as the rest of her features. Deepening what beauty there is she possesses. With a sigh pulled in unexhaled, she picks up her black book bag from the floor. With nary a glimpse toward Emily, she stands up straight again, gazing directly into Jennifer Lynn's eyes. Miranda wrinkles her mouth upon the quiet exhale, turning on the current of issues come and gone.

In full busty, blonde headed flair, she strolls away from this bizarre meeting of the minds, reluctantly leaving her friend alone with her enemy.

"It's obvious she doesn't like me very much," Jennifer says. Staring down at the private table.

"What is it between you two anyway? You were like, best friends or something."

Jennifer rests her elbows on the table, leaning her chin briefly, comfortably onto her hands clasped together. Emily notices behind her deep gray eyes a distant longing. A profound, indefinable sadness.

"Miranda and me were best friends in the sixth grade. And all the way through the sixth, seventh and eighth grade, we were inseparable. Then in my freshman year, Samantha Daley approached me on the first day of school. She convinced me to turn my back on Miranda. She made me stop speaking to her. I'll never forget the first time I walked past her and didn't say anything. I could feel how much it hurt her. But when I became a freshman cheerleader, Samantha, Kelly and Rosalyn just sort of pulled me into their inner circle. And I couldn't get out. Losing Miranda's friendship broke my heart, but I couldn't do a damned thing about it. Samantha and Kelly are just too damned rich and pretty. Rosalyn's being recruited to play volleyball by 10 different schools already and she's not even a senior. And she is as tough as Hell. She could probably be in a *gang* if she wanted. I'm telling you, with her doing whatever Samantha says, the rest of the girls in this school are *finished.* I'm not really even as good looking as they are but they always treat me like I am."

"You've got schools chasing you too," Emily says. "For gymnastics. And you know something? You *are* as pretty as they are. If you weren't, believe me, they would have ignored you. Just like they did me."

"But you're gorgeous, Emily. Why do you hide it in those clothes? No make up. You never smile. You don't do your hair. I mean, you're playing this Morticia Addams thing for all its worth."

"It's just who I am. I can't help it."

"Well, the whole school really is talking about you and Miranda, you know. They've seen you holding hands outside in all this rain. Somebody even said you were caught kissing in the bathroom. Is that true?"

"Of course it isn't. God, who said that?"

"Everybody," Jennifer says. "So what's up with that anyway? Are you two lovers or what?"

Emily's eyes are suddenly a prisoner of that mysterious, invisible force that lowers them, and makes it impossible for them to return a gaze.

"Oh. I see. Well, it doesn't matter anyway. They really are calling you Fire and Ice, you know. Pure steam, they say. And Hell, they're just jealous because they don't have a girl fuck buddy as pretty as y'all are."

"A girl *what?*"

"That's right. Half the girls in the whole damned school are fucking the other half behind their boyfriend's back, behind their Mom's back

271

and each other's back. You wanna hear a secret? One too dangerous to tell another living soul?"

Emily leans forward without a word, feeling as though an invisible magnet is at work toward her bowels and groin.

"Samantha has strapped it on, and fucked all three of us into submission. And she's not even gay."

"Are you serious?"

"As serious as Kelly's mom's bank account, baby. Two hundred and thirty thousand dollars in that thing."

"Are you kidding me?"

"And that is nothing compared to Samantha's mother. She is worth one point two *million* dollars."

Emily leans back in her chair, face stunned by anguish, properly slain by the power of secrets uncovered.

"How can anybody *compete* with that," Emily says, lips still parted in amazement.

"You can't," Jennifer says. "And you can't escape from it either. Look, I've got six brothers and sisters. My mother works in a factory, for God's sake. She hardly earns any money. You should see that little thing we live in called a house. So you see? I get it. I understand what it feels like to not be one of the rich girls. Because I'm actually *poor*."

"But you and Rosalyn both drive nice cars. And you've got plenty of money to spend."

"That's because Samantha's mom bought us those cars. And Samantha gives all three of us lots of money. She says we're her 'sisters in crime."

"Speaking of crime…Samantha told us that…that you four…"

"Raped the principal? Emily don't be ridiculous. She told you that because she knew you were already scared half to death because you knew she broke that J.V. cheerleader's arm. She told us you would believe it and she was right."

"You mean, you guys didn't have anything to do with that?"

Jennifer laughs again, smiling, hardly bothering to shake her head 'no' in response.

"I'm really sorry Emily. For all the fear and pain we caused you. Truth is, I've been worried about you since this whole thing got started. I want us to be friends."

"But what about Samantha?"

"Samantha hates your guts. But at least if I'm friends with you, she'll leave you alone."

"Are you sure?"

"If I wasn't, do you think I would be here?"

"I guess not."

"I can't take the way she's treating you anymore. And I told her so. Even if it meant my friendship with them, I wanted it to stop."

"And she's okay with this?"

"Actually, no. but for some reason, she wants me in. Bad enough to put up with it. And well, she actually said something funny when I told her."

"What'd she say?"

"She said, '*look, if you want to suck on that witch's cunt, I could care less. Just leave me the fuck out of it. I'm sick of your whining about it.*"

"She *said* that?" Emily says, smiling, on the edge of a laugh.

"You know she did. Truth is, I was afraid when I told her. I thought they were gonna beat me up."

"You didn't."

"I did. But she just took a deep breath and told me she couldn't care less."

"So what are we, like best friends now, or something?"

"Hardly, honey. I know as long as you and Miranda are a thing, that can't happen. But I want us to spend some time together. Because I want them to see that I'm serious about them leaving you alone. What happened in the cafeteria today… that wasn't supposed to happen. I had already talked to her."

"So *that's* why you acted so strange today."

"Like I said, I want her to stop. If she sees us together, she'll have to."

"But what if she cuts you off?"

"How can she cut off Jenny Lynn Johnson?"

And with that, Emily glances at the flash of confirmation in her brain, that delivers her a mighty reassurance, that nobody in this school, no man, woman, boy or girl, could turn their back on the most beautiful of all the kind hearted girls, state gymnastics finalist, and good Catholic girl they all knew.

Jennifer stands up from the table, coaxing the dark haired, goth pretty girl to her feet. Leaning across the table, the two of them share a tight, intimate hug and kiss on the cheek, the goth girl blissfully unaware of her new friend's sinister glance toward a nearby bookshelf, and her brief connection to the pair of beautiful eyes that stare.

Angel of Light

54

The rains of November have died down to a slow mist, as if pausing to take a breath in anticipation of what fiery trials may come. Emily is a willing passenger in silver Cadillac luxury, being driven through the cold mist as through a barrier; a wispy transcendence, a ghostly crossing over from melancholy and misery. The teenage dream of social acceptance, the ubiquitous desire to be embraced by the elite, this is the Angel of Light that beckons the brunette girl, as she is being driven through the gray, leaving the lonely dreariness of her blonde love behind for a day. Cruising the perimeter from fear and pain, toward the outer edge of the wilderness, to the horizon of joy and happiness born.

"I promise I'll protect you," are the words seeped into her spirit from Jennifer Lynn, words that soothe the pain away like medicine, and the fear like a warm fire in the icy cold. They ride along as though best friends, the two of them, the goth girl being driven along in the silver SUV of privilege, finding the big mall parking lot to get lost in.

In the lightness of spirits that bring complacency and hope for the future, Emily steps out of the SUV in the dying mist of rain, walking quickly with her sensual, beautiful new companion across the busy weekend parking lot, the two of them hurrying through the grand, glass doors into the mall entranceway, greeted by the sights, sounds and smells of retail Heaven on Earth. Her nose can hardly discern the triple threat that beckons—whether it be cheeseburgers, cheese Danish or cheese pizza that dominates each breath, to mingle with Icee cup and soft serve vanilla cone's lust of the eyes—to make her glad that she has chosen to hide her curves in loose clothing so she can eat.

"We'll get a big slice on the way out," her benefactor says as if reading her mind, leading them toward the center of this madness, past the sea of gumball machines and jewelry counters to the escalator, to where their stroll through the Macy's aisles awaits.

"This is definitely your world," Emily says. "I don't know if I should be here."

"Just relax," her friend says. "It's you and me today." And Emily watches and listens closely, to see if the echoes of bitterness and betrayal show through on every part of their little journey, but finding none that she can discern. She follows the capable, mature seventeen year old going on twenty four through every slick and shiny aisle and cozy, overpriced department of nothing—folded, boxed and hung in casual allure, gathering the requisite Elizabeth Arden boxes and bottles of magic to take home, where it will sit unsprayed for all eternity.

Jennifer embraces this Pygmalion spirit passed down, to make use of her new living doll to play with, stripping Emily of her faded black polo pullover and long black skirt and thrift store waist coat, to decorate her curves in the tightest black skinny jeans and black t-shirt and leather belt, with a pair of black pumps to boot. And she sees an opportunity to take this journey toward trust a step further, exchanging the pumps for a pair of leather boots, to suit the goth girl more appropriately, to highlight what spirit of dark and midnight Amazonia may rule.

And the both of them notice in the mirror, that among girls and women far and wide, Emily's shape is one of the most extraordinary examples; with big, wide hips that had been hidden for so long, but are now exposed in the fullness of feminine power and glory. And the tight, black t-shirt is exchanged for the black, longsleeved turtleneck shirt, to deliver this brunette in full, elegant goth form, where one of the curviest bodies ever formed is displayed in cloth the color of nighttime and pitch.

"I think you might have the biggest, prettiest ass I've ever seen on a white girl," Jennifer Lynn says, mouth open slightly in genuine reverence and awe. "When you wear this to school Monday, jaws are gonna *drop.*"

And the two of them leave the pretty aisles of Macy's world behind, to find their way to a makeup counter Jennifer says is the best but nobody believes it. They stroll through the pearly gates of Heaven at JC Penney, to the Sephora make up counter, to let irony in a thin man's body put the powder brushes and lipsticks onto the goth girl's pale face, even parting and brushing her hair to a more delicate autumn perfection, until the woman she sees in the mirror is barely recognizable to her, where sexy-prettiness is suddenly transformed before her eyes into sensual beauty.

"My God," the thin, handsome man says, so impressively effeminate, shaking his head, staring at the new exotic brunette in the mirror. "Wonder Woman," he says. Is it Italian or Greek?"

"Both," she says. "On my mother's side. Greek Italian farm girl," she was.

"Oh, I can *definitely* see that ," he says. "You were born in the wrong century, Isabella. To tell you the truth I'm sick of hearing that said about a woman every time she gets a makeover but honey, in your case..."

"I told you. James is an artist."

"Oh no. In faces honey, God is the artist. We just highlight what's already there. I'll never forget this one. Now go break some hearts, Sophia."

In the wake of this veiled prophecy given, the brunette exotic leaves the makeup counter, humbled by what she sees in the reflection, in nervous awe of the transformation from the frumpy, goth pretty to the shapely goth beauty she just saw in the mirror. Rising high on this cloud of confidence, and at least four inches of leather booted heel in tow, this ghost from 1888 walks in modern form beside her benefactor, who is suddenly paled to lovely mediocrity in comparison. They bypass the cheeseburgers and the cheese Danish, to sit at one of the tables where the cheese pizza is sealed in thin crust splendor. Jennifer Lynn talks and gazes in unpretend awe at the young woman across from her, whose gold hoop earrings contrast and highlight the hair as black as the raven's feathers, which falls about her shoulders and half the length of her back.

The pleasures of pizza, pretty smile bites and Mountain Dew delights their conversation, about the joys of the so-called in crowd, the cheerleader elite, and the love of money and privilege in the modern day. These two mature, sophisticated young girls have the last bites and sips of their delicious diversion, rising from their seats at the center of attention, Macy's and JC Penney shopping bags in hand, strolling the far end of the full circle, back past the Icee cup and soft serve vanilla cone signs, back to the glass doors, which now serve as an entrance into the grey world from whence they came.

They stroll into the brief pause between rains, the two of them, one in the spirit of protector and benefactor—the other in the spirit of hope and renewal. She is the kite flown in the color of pitch, touched in a fleck shard of gold shimmer, adrift in these winds of sad joy and melancholy happiness, the joyful sadness and happy melancholy born and nurtured, in grieving to be pulled back down to earth by the one who holds the string, by the blonde beauty, in whose veins flows the apocalyptic power of ice in crystalline form.

They place their bags in the back of Cadillac luxury in SUV, taking their pretty woman steps in gliding, as in a slow motion dream through the cold and gray, slipping inside their comfort cushioned chariot, complacent in latter day privilege and beauty.

And upon this final breath of distant melancholy breathed, at the precipice of joy unbridled, she feels a cold hand scratch and claw its way around her throat from behind, as the ghost of her waking nightmare appears in blonde, blue eyed beauty outside her window.

The hand of feminine power grips her throat from the back seat, at the moment complacency drains from her body in a wave of cold. As her breathing takes on the requisite, raspy tone, she looks out the window in wide eyed terror, beginning to tremble already, as though she were touched to her soul by a breath of winter. This blonde headed phantom, this demon opens the car door quickly, leaning its pretty head inside the car, close enough so that the scent of her mint candy breath is strong in her nostrils.

"Oh my," Samantha says, staring the exotic girl from her forehead to her chin. "I don't know whether to kill her... or fuck her."

The types of fear are many. And uniquely distinguished.

"You're dead, bitch," comes the voice from behind her, amidst the tightening of the strong, feminine grip at her throat. She turns the other way, trying to gather some last strand of hope, some last grain of faith in her benefactor.

"I'm sorry," Jennifer says. "I'm so sorry Emily…"

"Shut *up,* Jennifer," Samantha says. Touching her finger to Emily's chin. Turning the girl's face to hers. Gently.

Emily watches as her new mistress closes her eyes nearly all the way. Leaning closer to the deep red of her lips. Pressing her own lips to hers.

Gently.

The Twilight of Humanity

*T*his is one of the latter day places. A place replete with fear and sorrow. One of the darkest regions of shadow, in the twilight of humanity.

Somewhere in the grieving mist. In the cold Autumn rain that waits. These isolated roads along the Virginia countryside bear witness to tragedy. To the beginning of sorrows. To the eve of the Second Coming in power and glory.

These roads bear witness to a lonely traveler. A prisoner, if you will. Carried along these twilight roads in fear and grieving. This lonely prisoner, in the back seat of rolling silver luxury. With one girl on either side of her. Held tight between both girls, one from the homelife of violent shame. The other, a daughter of privilege and motherline hatred. These two of the four horsemen. The blonde leader, and her violent minded enforcer.

The enforcer stares boldly at her mistress and their victim. Watching her mistress kiss the brunette beauty, who receives every kiss in sorrow. Receiving every kiss in fear. Having to obey these quiet commands, even to the pushing of her tongue. The pushing of it into the blonde mistresses' mouth. Feeling the girl suck the light of hope from her soul.

From the pressing of lips to hers. From the pressures of fear and grieving. From this, the first tear is welled up into her vision. Rolling down the length of her beautiful face to the bottom. Causing her lips to tremble in the kiss. Rising a spark at the center of her breathing, until a single squeak of weakness, a single sob breaks forth from resistance. A sob that trembles her body. A break in the reservoir of tears and suffering. A break, causing a flood of sobs and shaking in her body. A flood of sobs during this kiss. Sobs that must take hold of her, to break this kiss ever so gently. So that her captor can hear her sorrow. So she can feel the breath of it on her lips.

The crying girl leans her head onto the blonde girl's shoulder. Her body shaking from the emotion. The other three girls listening intently. Gauging the nature of fear and pleasure. Of what it does to their fearful souls, to hear this strong, capable young woman broken down to nothing. Listening to her beg. Listening to her ask in tears and sorrow, of what manner of harm there must be. Having their spirits massaged to a place of involuntary arousal by the blonde's compassionate shushing. By her genuine comfort of the poor girl. Listening to the beautiful brunette sniff and squeak in her arms. Glimpsing the impossible mood of compassion from their mistress born.

Along this later day road. Through the waiting mist of rain they travel. Four in a growing mood of violence. The other, an inner pleading for mercy unspoken. A pleading too fearful to express. Clutching against the black collar shirt of her mistress captor. Pulling against the fabric in false hope. Pressing her lips to the blonde's cheek in desperation. Blessing Heaven in her heart, for the blonde's compassionate kiss on her forehead. For the soft stroking of the girl's hand across her hair.

In the mist of early twilight rain. In the cold of Autumn's turning toward the night. The rolling silver chariot finds its place along the flow of time. Along the flow of history. Rolling down the isolated path into a lost Virginia woods. Into a place of growing darkness and cold.

Please help me Samantha... please help me Samantha, comes the whining voice of reason. Comes the crying of a victim's better judgment. The pleading for mercy that has finally begun.

The rolling chariot finally stops at its destination. Somewhere in the backwoods of the Virginia countryside. Three of the girls open their doors, moving quickly out of the SUV. Leaving the two of them alone.

Don't let it happen to me Samantha. Please don't let it happen to me...

There's nothing I can do about it, baby. I'm sorry. It has to be this way. Just stay calm, and accept what has to happen. It'll all be over soon...

Firmly. Gently. The blonde begins to unbuckle the brunette's belt. Beginning to unbutton her black jeans. Pulling at her tight turtleneck top. Sliding it off with little difficulty. Stroking the brunette's hair back to a place of casual prettiness. Back to a place of sensual beauty.

In her bra, the brunette stares fearfully at the blonde. Feeling the spark of terror strike her soul, when the blonde's hand touches inside the front of her unbuttoned jeans. Inside the top of her underwear cloth still hidden. This spark of fear strikes, causing the brunette to turn hopelessly, sliding out of the car in the twilight mist. Powered along by the whining *no*'s of legend as she runs. Running pointlessly down the path from whence they came. Not knowing where in the world they have come from. Nor where in the world it is they may go. Running over the wet, woodsy ground in bra and boots, black pants barely undone. Slipping, stumbling over the wet ground. Falling. Feeling the weight of one slam heavily on top of her. Holding her down, while the others pull at her pants. Her boots. Her underwear cloth. Her bra. Feeling their scratching, clawing hands make quick work of her dignity as she kicks. As she screams.

The weight of cataclysm pins her to the forest floor. The weight of feminine strength in triplicate, holding her down heavily on her back. Holding her down as she holds her head back, screaming to the Heavens. Screaming the worlds *help me* to the uncaring trees. To the uncaring clouds. To every uncaring drop of rain.

The blonde approaches the three others in violence. Unzipping her jeans. Pulling out the extension of herself strapped on. The burning of blue and black fire.

This is one of the latter day places. A place of twilight and misery.

The blonde lowers herself to the ground. Crawling herself between the others laid on the naked brunette's arms and legs. Pushing her fingers deep inside her. Feeling the energy of new screams. The power of a death scream.

The blonde takes the extension of herself in her hand. Guiding it to its proper place. Its improper place. Pushing every inch of it inside the screaming young woman. Pressing her hand over the girl's mouth. To relish the muffled scream in her hands. To hear it in the air around her. To feel it in both her body and soul.

Every thrust builds energy upon itself. To power a new thrust within. To guide her hips forward to their destination. Then by instinct, to stop her movements at the moment of truth. To let this train coast the limits of its calling. To let the feeling in her groin explode of its own volition. To open her mouth, and let this Armageddon Call erupt in a shriek for the ages. An angry warrior's cry from deep within. A yell that trembles mightily from her body's shaking. From the quaking thundered from her head to her feet.

The blonde lays there. Slipping her hand away from the brunette's mouth. Listening to her hoarse screams and yelling die down to a tragic whimpering. A whimpering of false hope reborn. Erroneous beliefs of a reprieve nurtured and grown.

In the latter day mist of rain. In the oppressive truth on open display. The blonde girl raises up from her victim. Giving the final order of the day. As the earth turns toward the evening. Watching them guide the naked girl through the rest of her trip over this part of the timeline. Watching them guide her to where the black plastic covers an upright place. Where more black plastic covers a lower place around the upright.

The blonde begins the last part of their journey through this part of time. Sliding, pulling all of the black plastic away from the upright wooden stake driven into the ground. From the sticks of wood kept dry from the grieving weather scattered around. She watches, as the other three horsemen move their naked victim to her destiny. Binding her in rope to the wooden stake driven firmly in. Clicking the lock on the chain around her neck pulled tight. Positioning the dry wooden sticks around the naked girl again. Watching her strained, exhausted pleas go unheard by them. Unheralded by the spirits of the approaching night.

Ice

The blonde watches her slaves throw the fuel onto the dry sticks. Splashing it hurriedly by many gallons. Coating the naked girl from her hair to the toes of her bare feet. Knowing that where the will of man ends is a mystery. Knowing only the future striking of a flame.

The blonde pours a heavy line of fuel a distance away. Striking a match in the growing mist of rain. Bending to the wet ground, touching it to the woodsy grass. Watching it flash a rapid line across the twilight ground to the fuel soaked sticks of wood. Awestruck as the wood explodes in a burst of orange fire and vapour of smoke. Shocked by the nature of death in the human voice. By the force of screaming made possible. By the name of the Lord himself screamed to the heavens in the twilight.

This is one of the latter day places. A place replete with fear. With pain.

With death.

Jonathan Lovejoy

The Rains from

Melancholy Bay

The rains from Melancholy Bay have returned with a steady assurance, to remind the world that there is still an infinity of rain and grief to bear. Miranda stands at the window of her nighttime bedroom, watching the procession of strange lightning flashes in this autumn storm, hearing at least once that sometimes, every so often, there is thunder in a November rain.

These low, unusual rumblings pull my attention away from my internet browsing, away from the memories of my failed marriage, and acceptance of my mediocre life, drifting me down the upstairs hall to my daughter's room.

"Did Emily say she was going to be this late?"

"No. She didn't say when she was coming home. I'm so worried about her Mom. It's a bad feeling in the pit of my stomach."

As if inspired by her grief and worry, a bolt of lightning flashes angrily in the clouds, glowing like a white filament plugged in.

Quietly.

"Hurricanes do this," I say. "They happen in November. But the news says this is just a regular thunderstorm, *"of hurricane-like energy and duration,"* they said. Even they said the lightning and thunder is not normal in a rainstorm this time of the year."

Miranda is unable to answer. Unable to concentrate on anything not focused on her brunette friend and lover.

"She'll turn up, honey. Quit worrying."

"You don't understand, Mom. Those four girls are the biggest bitches in the state of Virginia. They are all shallow, self absorbed *witches,* who get off on hurting people weaker than they are. None of them can be trusted. Not even Jennifer."

"The one you used to play with? Jenny Lynn Johnson?"

"That's her."

"And you think that somehow, she's trying to hurt you through a new friendship with Emily?"

"It's more than that," Miranda says. "I think… I think they want to hurt Emily. In the worst way."

"How so?"

"I mean really hurt her. Physically."

"You mean like… like beat her up or something?"

"At least that. Maybe something worse."

My attention is drawn back to her nighttime window, by another flash of pure energy in the storm. I now understand why her lights are off, except for the faint glow coming from the hallway through the open door.

"Is that why you're standing in here in the dark? Because you're worried about Emily?"

"Yes and no. I do this a lot now, since it started raining through the night. I can see the lightning better when its dark."

I go over to where my daughter stands still at the window, as if frozen by grief and worry.

"If she loves you," I say, hugging her around the waist from behind. She'll be back."

"Thanks a lot, Mom," she says, her voice rich with sarcasm. "That *really* makes me feel a lot better."

"I'm serious, Miranda. You don't think those girls are going to hurt Emily any more than I do. You're just scared that she's going to abandon you."

As Miranda turns her head slightly toward me, a third wire of pure, electrical power shows itself so mysteriously, so enigmatically in the storm. What follows is the loudest boom and rumbling we have heard so far, rattling our insides through the roof and the walls of our little suburban palace, rolling with purpose over the rainsoaked nighttime Virginia countryside.

The shadows of worry haunt Miranda for the rest of the weekend, pressing down on her, creating enough pressure to drive her to action. This, being an unwanted trip through the rain and misery to the working class neighborhood of Jennifer Lynn Johnson herself, the girl who supposedly had taken Emily under her wing for protection.

"What do you mean she *went home?*"

"She started talking about you, and how she felt like she was betraying you for 'doing this,' whatever that means. And I said, 'doing what?' And she said 'becoming close friends with you after the history you two have. Since Samantha came between you.' So, I took her home after we left the mall yesterday afternoon. She didn't call you from her house?"

"No. Why would she go home? She was staying at my house."

"I asked her that. She said she felt the need to make up with her Mom, and that she was gonna call you. You haven't heard from her?"

Standing at the door of Jennifer Lynn's livingroom, enduring the curious glances from two of her four sisters, Miranda brushes her blonde hair back over her ear, attempting a smile through the bewilderment.

"I dropped her off a few blocks from her house. She said she wanted to walk in the rain for a few minutes and clear her head. You know how much she likes to walk in the rain."

"Yeah," Miranda says, taken aback by the audacity in Jennifer Lynn's expression. "I *do* know that."

And from this, Miranda is inspired to leave Jennifer Lynn behind without as much as a glance goodbye. To drive to her friend's house, even stopping a block away, to make the strange trip in her mind, along her friend's ghostly trail, until she stands at the front door of revelation. Where the third part of the truth reaches out to her through Ms. Watson's voice, gripping her insides with a cold even she can feel.

"The little whore hasn't been here. And to tell you truth, I don't give a damn where she is. If you find her, keep her."

And when the door of this revelation closes, it does so on the opening of a new pain in Miranda's life, where she suddenly has to deal with a loss she is unprepared to confront.

As she walks away from what was once Emily's home, the pain of bewilderment threatens to morph already into grief and confusion. To torment her young mind, body and emotions, creating a stress somewhere beyond her nerves, down deep past every muscle and bone, causing what cold she feels in this autumn rain to dissipate.

Reaching her hand out from underneath her umbrella as she walks, she notices the drops of cold rain are *warm* to her touch, and her breath suddenly appears as an icy fog in the air around her. Of what mysterious and unearthly energy this is, of what growth and power she feels, she does not know, only that as she walks past the fire hydrant on the corner, she knows that she need not reach down and touch it with her hands. She backs up a bit, still under her umbrella by natural instinct, staring at the hydrant in focused, deep concentration, until it appears enveloped in a flow of rising *steam* from all over it, as the air around it is transformed to icy cold…

And this bizarre process moves along, until the metal from the hydrant begins to morph into something *frozen,* into something tragic and brittle, until it breaks apart in a great noise, making her turn her eyes away in astonishment and fear.

In the falling rain, among the sea of raindrops pouring downward, there is a fountain explosion from the neighborhood city street, blowing a column of water taller than a two story house, rising the height of a telephone pole into the air. And much to her own curiosity, the blonde girl under the umbrella is compelled to stare at this water tower with nary a blink, until the rushing water ceases to be, and the tower of white water is suddenly smooth and sculpted from the bottom to the top, fashioned in the form of a crystal fountain frozen in time.

Jonathan Lovejoy

Where the Goblins Go

*F*rom the crystal fountain born from revelation. To the hallways of fruitless learning bye and bye, Miranda walks through the school in a haze of the same, fearful misery she had felt all weekend. Having already made the police aware of Emily's disappearance, but getting nothing to even vaguely resemble a commitment from them to find her.

"Believe me, Ms. Auburn, she'll turn up. They always do. It sounds like she just decided to run away. And there's no telling where in the world she is. You say her and her mother didn't get along? Classic runaway. When she runs out of money for cabs and cheap motels in a few days, she'll come running right back to you…"

Ice

Miranda drifts the halls of the school in this selfsame disillusionment, the same echo of despair she had already felt before, wondering where it is that her friend and lover could have gone. *She'll like the frozen fountain*, Miranda thinks, unable to dismiss the possibility of a return as sudden and mysterious as her departure.

"I see the ice," comes a voice from behind her at her locker, "but where's the fire?"

Miranda turns around from her open locker, startled by the smiling face of her lovely tormentor.

"Where's your friend, Miranda?" Samantha says, the beautiful Kelly standing beside her, sucking a bubble gum bubble noisily back into her pretty mouth.

"Maybe I should ask *you* where she is, Samantha."

"Now how would I know where Witch Hazel went when Jennifer dropped her off. I tried to warn Jennifer that your precious *Emily* was a weird flake but she didn't want to hear it. And now, the weirdo is gone. And nobody knows where she went. She probably just got a head start on it, that's all."

"On what?"

"On her life as a homeless bag lady, what else?"

Miranda watches helplessly, as the two of them erupt in screaming, cackling laughter.

"Samantha I always knew you were cruel, but I had no idea—"

"No, honey. You don't," she says, the laughter suddenly draining from her lovely features. Miranda notices that Samantha's mature, sensual beauty is well beyond her years.

"Samantha, why are you so *mean?* You've got everything. You're beautiful. You're smart. You're rich. So why do you have to pick on people that are weaker than you are?"

"Like who? Like your friend Witch Hazel? It was her who started this, remember? That bitch got me suspended because of a little handwritten note attached to her locker. A little note that basically called it like I saw it."

"She is not a *witch.* Why do you keep calling her that?"

"Can I help it if she comes to school every day dressed like something out of a Tim Burton movie?"

"But what business is it of yours how she chooses to dress? Why do you torment her for being different?"

"I torment her for being stupid. For being stupid enough to think she can challenge *me.* To think she can come anywhere *near* me with her disrespectful bullshit. *Nobody* does that to me and gets away with it. And the only thing protecting you? Is the fact that you used to worship Jennifer before I came along. And rescued her from growing into a pathetic loser like you."

Samantha's expression twists in genuine disgust, as she stares Miranda down from her blue eyes to her big bosom.

"If you hurt her Samantha. If you hurt her I swear to God…"

"That you'll do what? Breast bump me to death? I bet you'd like that wouldn't you? Both of us stripped down to our underwear bottoms. Our *panties.* Hands behind our back. Using our *tits* to try and push each other off balance. And the whole time… wishing you could shove one of those big things in my mouth."

Ice

Miranda glances over at Samantha's beautiful friend, noticing her gazing slack jawed, with nary a motion on her bubble gum to be found. As if waiting for her to speak. To answer.

"So, you just better watch your step, tit queen. Or should I say, *Ice* Queen."

"Ice *cream*," Kelly says. Casting a strong, sensuous gaze.

"Down girl," Samantha says. Smiling. "You'll get your chance."

"In your *dreams*," Miranda says.

"And there she is," says Samantha. "Miss Ice Queen. With a frozen stick up her pretty little ass. Thinks she's too good for the rest of us girls. Sorry Kelly. It looks like the only head sleeping on those pillows... is gone."

"Where has she gone, Samantha? I *know* you know. *Please* tell me."

"She's gone... where the *goblins* go... bitch."

The breath of this last syllable touches Miranda's lips, as Samantha speaks close to her mouth, staring her directly in the eye. The class bell screams its warning to them in the empty hall, as Samantha holds her dark gaze into Miranda's eyes, turning when the tolling of the bell ends, strolling with her beautiful slave to somewhere else in God's creation.

he rest of Miranda's school day is spent in the spirit of fear. Moving from hour to hour with a certain looking over her shoulder, as if chased through this part of the timeline by a cold, icy dread. Between every class, she looks around with every step to her locker, every step to the next class, enduring a spark of pure nervousness every time she glimpses either one of the four horsemen. Wanting so desperately at the lunch hour to make the journey across a crowded room, to the table where the four of them sit at the top of their game, as the four rulers of this high school kingdom.

Two major obstacles in their path have been apparently done away with; one, the sexy pretty principal. Whether or not these four actually did the crime, Miranda can feel that somehow, their energy exudes an evil presence, a power that reaches out from them, to do whatever dreadful bidding they desire. And two—the sudden and mysterious disappearance of her soulmate, her friend and lover, the only other human being beyond her mother that she could ever come to terms with, could ever have a connection and understanding with, beyond the superficial, and the fleeting bye and bye. And she is amazed at the lack of concern for Emily's whereabouts from every teacher she talks to, and from every student as well.

In the matter of Emily Watson, Miranda Auburn is alone.

The hours move Miranda along the space of this part of her earthly journey, building pressure onto all of her senses, until school and schoolwork begin to fade to insignificance. Knowing that at the end of this fifth period history, sixth period would have to be done away with today. After this brief eternity through the whitewashing of some world event or another, Miranda hurries past the others in their pointless meandering, moving quickly toward the classroom where Jennifer Lynn will emerge from. And it seems that the line of students coming out of the chemistry class files onward to near infinity, until she wonders if Jenny Lynn has not chosen to skip it and go to the mall with the other three. But at that moment, the nature of fear sparks a cold and icy touch to her heart, when Jenny Lynn Johnson strolls in full blown, womanly appeal, looking as though she were truly one of the untouchables, one of the unobtainable few among them. Miranda hurries over to this sexy bottomed girl, taking firm hold of her upper arm, enough to make Jennifer turn to look at her in brutal, confused judgment and bewilderment.

"What are you *doing?"*

"I need to talk to you."

"No... let go of my arm... God, Samantha was right, your hands *are* cold... I said let *go* of me."

But the strength and power in Miranda's grip serves only to push Jennifer toward the other side of resistance. In the calm of this uneasy acceptance, Miranda begins to escort the frustrated, brown haired beauty through the sea of curious glances, a few of them already aware of the simmering drama threatening between these two. Miranda walks calmly, quietly escorting Jennifer all the way down the hall, past both their classes—down the hall and around the corner, to a more far away exit.

Miranda pushes against the big, metal bar across the door with her body, clicking the door noisily open, moving them both out of the afternoon crowd and outside under the long, concrete walkway, sheltering them both from the cold, autumn rain.

"I already told you, I *don't* know where the Hell she is."

"How stupid do you think I am, Jennifer? I know you guys were planning to do something to her, and I *begged* her not to go. And now you've got her trapped somewhere in some horrible, God forsaken place and you better tell me where or so help me God…"

"And you'll do what, Miranda? Baby, you better back off. Because you're in enough trouble as it is…"

"What is that supposed to mean? Back off of what?"

"Of *us*," she says. "And just face facts, Miranda. That for now, Emily is gone. And we don't know where she is."

As if hearing a voice from somewhere, from somewhere beyond her mind and body, Miranda glances toward the Great Looking Away, breathing a deep breath in surrender, upon which her hand reaches out as if on its own power, taking firm, strong hold of the beautiful teenage woman, escorting her through the rain, toward where her destination is inevitable on this part of the journey.

"Let go of my arm you ice handed *freak*…I said let go of me you crazy…"

After their brief trek through the autumn cold, they arrive at the place where water sports is king, and whose time has nearly arrived for another season. In this auditorium, far across the school lawn, they go into the still abandoned entrance area, Miranda pulling Jennifer Lynn roughly along, ignoring the constant echo of her voice in the empty building.

In effortless strength, in the power of her easy command, she pulls her former friend along without mercy, opening the door to the inner sanctuary, dragging Jennifer toward the large, empty swimming pool.

With nary a word, and without hesitation, Miranda uses what otherworldly strength her mind can conjure, tossing the mature, teen beauty in a brief, rainbow arc, splashing her *hard* into the water.

In the requisite choking. The proverbial coughing voice. The girl finds the breath she needs, to sputter a promise into the air around her.

"We're gonna get you expelled for this you crazy *bitch!*"

"Where is she?"

"Fuck you!"

And upon this evil, wet haired defiance, the girl turns to swim toward the metallic steps, to climb her way to cold, wet victory. But upon touching the silver rails, the water around her begins to splash and wave, seeming to follow her up to the top of her climb, until unbeknownst to her, a space of clear water in the form of a *woman* rises up from below, grabbing her around the head with its watery arm, pulling her hard and backwards into the pool, splashing her deep and twisting beneath the surface.

After a dreadful, choking moment under the water, Jennifer pokes her head up as high as she can, stealing a breath of precious hope and delusion.

"Help! Help!"

This, she screams with fever, her voice echoing from the rafters, until she slowly realizes that the beautiful blonde haired girl, kneeling on one knee at the side of the pool, has end of the world business to tend to.

"How are you doing this? Samantha is right you're *witches!*"

And in the wake of this, this stubborn refusal to give in, a shimmering, crystal clear hand rises from the water, to burst forth another series of screams like a fountain. The hand lowers back into the water, leaving a whirlpool in its wake the size of a full grown woman.

"She's *DEAD!*"

The types of fear are many. And uniquely distinguished.

"What... what did you say?"

"You heard me, she's *dead!* Samantha burned her *alive!* She raped her and then she burned her in the *woods!*"

And suddenly, the ghostly sound Miranda hears is that of her own voice, whispering the front edges of a long whine, destined to grow into a cataclysmic shriek of pure horror.

What is the third part of the truth?

Cataclysm.

Along the current of this soft, wailing moan, Miranda slips back onto the floor in sitting, sliding backward just a bit, as if trying to push away from this revelation, the truth of what happened to her friend and lover, of her fiery death in a cold, lonely Virginia woods, leaving her lost and alone in a gray, condemned world, to wonder for an eternity where it is that her beloved Emily could have gone.

Seizing this moment, she swims to the silver railing, climbing out, clothes dripping wet to the floor. With a fearful, bewildered glance at the pool, Jennifer nearly stumbles her way to where Miranda sits back on her hands, her face frozen in pain and fear.

"I don't know how you did that, but you better *stay away from me!* Or I swear to God, I'll make sure you get that same thing she got!"

Miranda is unable to move a muscle, still a prisoner of shock and terror, helplessly watching the wet headed beauty walk in confused frustration toward the door.

"You just wait until Samantha hears about this," she says. Turning an evil gaze to the helpless blonde on the floor. And just as before, a calm of surrender overtakes Miranda in completion, turning her mind to the question of pre-ice molecules and how they move, causing a great disturbance again in the pool, a splashing noise which freezes Jennifer Lynn in her tracks just long enough to turn and see the *water witch* rise completely out of the pool, the top half of her in greater form of a shimmering crystal clear woman of water this time, stretching from the bottom of herself still attached to the water inside the massive swimming pool.

The ice cold spirit splashes herself into the screaming, wet haired beauty with force and power, slamming her violently against the outer doors briefly, gathering her up and levitating her above the floor on the return trip, reforming herself as a woman of death by water, diving the wet haired beauty back into the pool, twisting her like a boat propeller this time, then holding her still, gathering herself in full, crystal clear feminine form beneath the water, her arms wrapped tightly around the struggling, hopeless Catholic girl.

Miranda moves slowly, crawling herself to the edge of the swimming pool, touching the surface of the water with the palm of her hand. As her breath appears in fog, the shimmering around her hand is replaced by crystalline stillness, in the sound of a creaking noise that echoes, while the crystalline stillness spreads from one side of the water to the other. In less than a minute's time, the surface of the entire pool is coated in crystal clear *ice,* where the terrified form of the wet haired girl can be seen, rising to the surface underneath the water, pushing in false hope against the clarion truth of what she sees.

On her hands and knees, Miranda watches the girl underneath the water, floating violently toward her, kicking wildly, screaming bubbles in muffled sound above her head. Miranda watches closely, locked into this horror, to study the nature of fear and death.

And at the moment of truth, she leans as far forward as she can, to witness the palms of the girl's hands press flat against the frozen surface, as her wide eyes go blank, as the bubbles pouring from her open mouth are ceased to be.

In the aftermath of trauma. In the wake of latter day tragedy. Miranda Auburn rests on her hands and knees, her body racked with end of the world sobbing, screaming the name of the girl she loves past the roof of the auditorium. Through the rain. Into the grieving gray clouds.

And beyond.

Jonathan Lovejoy

In the Cold of the Rainy Autumn Night

61

*I*n the working class suburb of Rosalyn Reynolds. In the grieving cold of this rainy November night. There is the lovely white hand stretched forth, from the mysterious figure dressed in black, in the cold of the rainy autumn night. In the wee hours of the morning, long past the stroke of midnight's due, this lovely white hand touches the front door of this suburban home in the rain, holding the doorknob until it is frosted over in tragedy. Touching the other lovely white hand to the deadbolt lock so-called, until this self same frosting over is achieved.

After but a moment, the hands push against the door of security long gone, the door of security passed to oblivion, pushing this door over the sound of a crackling noise in the night. The figure in black, head covered in hooded protection from the rain, gazes briefly the jagged remains of metal and wood transformed to the substance of icy brittleness, where only the mild pushing of the door causes access to their den of safety. Metal and wood transformed, as if touched by something beyond liquid nitrogen, to produce the brittleness of a brick carved from powdered snow.

Past this mysterious reality, this figure walks quietly into the strange, middle of the night dwelling, following every unfamiliar sight and smell to the bottom of the carpeted stairs, climbing them with nary a nerve nor hesitation, to the hallway of the nighttime upper rooms. Feeling the substance of protection and guidance along this journey. Along this path toward vengeance that must be.

Opening the nighttime doors to two of the four bedroom doors she thinks she sees, where the strong and beautiful mother lies asleep in blue collar exhaustion; where the older sister lies dead to the world in this selfsame misery, opening the door to the third bedroom at last, walking calmly inside.

This figure dressed in black removes the hood from its head, to reveal the substance of blondeness. The power of blue eyes that stare. This blonde figure reaches down to the sleeping tough girl, the enforcer, slowly uncovering her, sliding her linen from her body to the foot of the bed. And she watches as the sleeping girl realizes that what she senses in her sleep is not the substance of a dream, causing her to open her eyes suddenly in half sleep, opening her mouth to try and breathe a word of warning in the air. Perhaps, a scream. To wake up the rest of her family, so that together they can descend on this intruder like a pack of wolves on a wayward fawn in the woods.

But at the moment her mouth is open, the blonde slams her hand over her mouth, clamping it down shut, which seems to burn her face with a cold unimaginable. She lies pinned on her back, as if held by invisible hands, while the blonde stranger holds her hand still and tight, until it feels as though her teeth are imbedded in a regretful bite into an icy snow cone, unable to open or close her mouth a millimeter's width, and unable to see the tragedy of what is there, when the stranger slides her hand away, to reveal the smooth, frosted surface where before lips and an open mouth had been.

The blonde holds this girl down on her back. Watching the fear and rage in her eyes do a dance of death, listening to the girl's muffled screaming come out through her nose. The blonde holds her immobile without effort, gathering her hatred nerve, sliding her hand to the screaming girl's throat...

The blonde grips her firmly around her neck, allowing the energy in her body to travel through, until she sees the girl on her back look somewhere beyond the ceiling, her muffled screams morphing into a high pitched scream unrealized, as her body becomes still and stiff as a board, from the top of her head to the soles of her feet.

*I*n the upper middle class suburb of Kelly LeMonde. Under this selfsame cloak of a rainy Autumn's night. This figure in black traverses the wee hours of this journey, having crossed over to another part of town. Convinced this time of the ease of their back patio door. Watching the so-called glass turn quickly into something more easily dealt with, nearby the door handle. She pushes through this icy transformation, undeterred by the soft plinking of crystals on the darkened kitchen floor inside, reaching through the small hole created in the big glass, unlocking the door with ease.

She slides the patio door open in the dark, pushing past the elegant curtain pulled shut. Walking slowly through this second, more profoundly unfamiliar space, guided by these same spirits of the vengeance that must be. Moving stealthily through the dark living room décor—upper class luxury hidden in the deathly hours after midnight. Turning slowly to the waiting staircase, making quick work of each one of them to the upstairs hall.

By Predestiny's whim, she bypasses the first door on this trip, drawn by an instinct unbeknownst, knowing by attrition what door to go to in the suburban dark. And just as she had somehow known and understood, this door opens into a celebration in the dark, where the ribbons and trophies and fake diamond tiaras decorate the chamber of obsession, the place where beauty worship is queen.

She stands over the sleeping beauty in the darkness, watching, listening to her draw every condemned breath in her sleep. She is compelled to reach underneath the lampshade, to bring the scene of this deed to a greater purity—clicking on the lamp, struck by the mature, sensual beauty on the face of this living doll.

The blonde ghost slides the covers from her lovely victim, impressed by the generous curves revealed, of the failed beauty queen, whose inheritance had taken over her body, and kept her from starving herself thin to please her mother.

As this shapely beauty breathes a sleeping sigh, the blonde leans down to her face, pressing her lips to hers in a kiss, holding it there, waiting for the sleeping beauty to awaken. In but a moment, across the ticking of a few seconds through time, the gorgeous young woman opens her eyes into instant shock, beginning to kick and push helplessly against the young blonde woman engaged in this unwanted kiss, this kiss that fills her body with terror, and the sudden echo of freezing cold.

Through her nose, she draws a breath, to give power to the screams stored within, writhing under the grip of this blonde girl's impossible strength, screaming her muffled tragedy into the girl's mouth without ceasing. And it seems that every breath she draws in is colder than the last, and harder to exhale into her muffled scream, until at last, the warm breath in her body is replaced with uncompromising cold, a cold she cannot push out on her own, but which only flows out through her nose in a ghostly whining sound. As an icy feeling traverses her body through and through, making it impossible for her to move. The kissing blonde holds her mouth in place, until every part and particle of the bedroom beauty lies still, and paralyzed in the aftermath of deep and abiding cold.

Jonathan Lovejoy

Hell's Angel

63

*I*n the upper class suburb of Samantha Daley. Among the houses of brick and brass fixture splendor. Where the spaces between the houses are vast and telling, that these are the homes of privilege. Houses spaced into earthly comfort by divine luck. Where credit scores and charisma are no substitute for capital. The place where savings and income are king and queen.

Ice

This is a predestined stroll through rain world. Along the privileged streets of this part of the condemned landscape. Rains that have decided to echo the days of Noah, where six weeks of tragedy fell from the skies without ceasing. Done in a latter day's warning, a latter day's grief and mourning. To allow the rainbow promise to be kept ad infinitum, that forty days of torrential rainfall in one little corner of the world is nothing. Forty days of rain that cannot widen a single river beyond this downpour. That cannot fill a single lake to overflowing anywhere beyond the borders of this little autumn rainstorm. Rain that cannot burden the continental shores with the rising of a single inch of ocean water. A unique and powerful burst of grief from the clouds, settling over the town of Richland Hills, Virginia for now. Rain fallen from the arm of energy swirled far across the eastern Virginia landscape, to the beaches of the cold and dreary Atlantic. An autumn rain of protracted, melancholy endurance and power.

In this downpour of suffering. In the splashing of autumn cold from the sky. As the flashes of light begin to decorate the bottom of these clouds in tributaries of white tinted blue. There emerges from the grandest house among them a woman of youth. A seventeen year old queen. Whose spirit inhabits the body of one much older. A spirit *and* body at least seven years beyond the age of this vessel. The spirit of adult maturity, burdening a young mind and body to conform.

This sensual, self satisfied young woman switches shapely hips from side to side toward SUV luxury. A strong, blonde woman of means. Set to inherit a million dollar trust within the year.

The young woman is barely startled, when a flash of morning lightning reveals a figure dressed in black, stepping from the side of her mini-mansion home. Gliding toward her in cloak and hooded mystery.

The figure steps around the front of the silver Mercedes. Joining the blonde woman under her umbrella. Lowering her head. A collision of blonde, blue eyed worlds in the storm.

"Where did you leave her?" the ice blonde asks.

And upon this question, rests the depth of the fire blonde's apocalyptic heart and bravery.

"After I fucked her," she says, "I burned her. And I left her in the woods to *rot.*"

She watches the affect this fiery hammer has in the cold, as the ice blonde breathes in a breath she cannot deny, shaking her head 'no' once in the effort.

"Oh yes," the fire blonde says. "Believe it."

"Do you... do you have the *balls*... to show me?"

"Why not," she says, gazing the ice queen from her silver blonde hair, to her lips as pink as the rose.

"Get in. I'll take you there."

The silver blonde strolls to the other side of the silver chariot, pushing, pressing through the pain. Climbing inside with the Hell's Angel.

With nary a word beyond a cruel snicker and glance, the girl slides the first of her traveling songs into her disc player, to remind her passenger of who the real deal is at Amber West High School, and who really is *Insane in the Brain.* This, followed quickly by the latter day suburban girl anthem, that declares once and for all, to the end of the age that 'I am entitled because yes, baby, I'm *Worth It.*'

Across the fields of plenty, they travel. Past the rainsoaked forests and fields of the autumn landscape, beyond the reach of the mothers and fathers of dead and naïve concern, who have relegated parenthood to glorified autopilot, where the children's morality is shaped and formed by the state, by the movie house, by the concert stage, and every vulgar and X Rated effort in between.

They roll on past the lonely farmhouses of dark secrets hidden in the latter day, where the modern mother daughter dynamic flourishes in the shadows, like a night rose in full bloom. They roll onward. On past the homes of bruises and blood, punctuated by the agony of a broken bone or two. They roll on past these fields of enmity, to a place where the woods grow at the base of a mountain chain—where the forest leaf canopy gives shelter to every pain, and every secret buried within.

They turn off the main road into a netherworld. A place where the road is a glorified path of flattened grass and wood lawn, leading deep into a thick woods, which opens up into a vast clearing, where the grasses are barely weighted down in the cold, autumn rain. And in the morning light of this clearing, as Beethoven's song of sorrow mourns as *The Emperor* of lamentations for piano and orchestra, the passenger glimpses the charred remains of an upright stick surrounded by burned wood, and the presence of something chained to it in the form of ashes and death.

"The whole world's gonna be talking about what happened to Jennifer at the pool," she says. "I guess you really are a witch. Like your friend was."

The ice blonde is unable to resist the shock, the cold wave blown through by this end of the world audacity. Turning to glimpse at the insane girl for a moment, she opens the door to get out of the SUV into the grieving weather, feeling the driver's strong grip on her upper arm.

"You and me together," she says…"would be the end of the world."

The ice blonde can only brave the rest of the cold wave washed through, pulling away from the fire blonde's burning grip—moving out into the cold, autumn mist in the grassy clearing, seeing that there are the burned, wet remains of what was once a living, breathing woman of hope and love. She stumbles through the morning mist, her hand over her mouth in disbelief, reaching out to touch the burned face of this thing, receiving a spark of confirmation in her spirit that yes, the dead are corrupted, and accursed above ground in the land of the living.

"So how 'bout it Miranda," comes the voice of fallen womanhood from the air around her. "Are you with me… or the dead girl?"

She takes one last, long stare into the face of a life come and gone, turning in total surrender to this predestiny, in submission to what must be. She removes her cloak, then begins to undo the rest of her clothing, calming her foe, her victim, into the battle mode of her dreams.

In but a moment, the two girls are in their bra cloth and underwear, standing still to face each other in the icy mist, and the realization that for one of them, death will come in the cold, Virginia woods this morning.

The ice blonde moves toward the fire maiden, raising her hand to grip the woman's throat, but only to the avail of feminine power and skill, as the fire blonde grips her wrist and arm, flipping her over mightily, slamming her to the wet grass of the forest clearing. Then, she brings her knee down in full into the ice maiden's stomach, to elicit a sickening yelp, then twisting herself, pulling the ice queen's arm out straight— wrapping her legs around her neck while pulling her arm, causing her to scream in agony to the clouds.

At the edge of an elbow popped loose from its socket, the maiden's entire arm takes the character of absolute, biting cold, which burns the fire maiden's bare skin in the rain, causing her to scream once and let go as if she were bitten by a serpent.

"What kind of a freak are you?" she says. Standing to her feet, backing up slowly, her arms crossed over the pain on her abdomen. "Your arm was so cold it felt like you electrocuted me."

But the ice maiden steps forward undeterred, unmoved by the fear and shock on the fire queen's beautiful expression.

"I'm leaving your freaky ass here," she says. "And I'm gonna tell the cops what you did to Jennifer…"

But at the instant she tries to open the SUV door, a powerful gust of ice cold wind whirls her away, slamming her to the ground more than 10 feet away. The fire blonde stands slowly to her feet, in full, black bra and underwear splendor, hips exposed like a gymnast in the high cut bottoms, staring in fearful surrender at the great breasted maiden in white bra cloth, who steps toward her in feminine form of the ages, a body passed down from the mother of all living.

Fight or flight must take its solemn hold in crisis, powering her body to turn and run with smooth, athletic prowess from the clearing toward the grassy car trail, believing that escape to the main road is imminent. But the sound of whispering winds blow a warning through the rain

327

soaked autumn trees, making her turn in time to see the outstretched hands of an ice phantom, a misty form of a *snow ghost* in the rain, reaching out to grab the fleeing girl in its icy grip, pushing her face first to the wet forest floor, grabbing her by the legs, dragging her screaming on her back toward the ice maiden who watches, her hair blowing wildly in the breeze—and to the fire maiden's horror, with eyes glossed over the color of moonlight in the wind.

In the rising of a new scream, in the throes of a death scream wrought for the spirits that stare, she is held immobile down on her back, as the snow phantom vanishes, and the ice maiden kneels, crawling slowly in the power of this easy command, until she is on all fours on top of the screaming girl held invisibly down beneath her.

The ice maiden lowers herself onto the fire maiden, feeling the girl's screams of terror reverberate into the forest tree canopy nearby, laying herself flat down in full on her body, groin to groin, waist to waist, breast to breast. Laying there in full dominance, pinning the maidens arms tightly to her sides, the girl's legs laid straight out on the ground in pure terror.

She lays on top of the screaming girl, watching her, feeling her sanity give way to every type of fear coalesced, until the ice maiden feels the wave of power appear in her flesh all its own, moving into the screaming maiden in a bolt of pleasure unfathomable, causing the ice queen to have to hold her head back in a grimace of strength, to correspond to the fire queen's head held back against the ground in wide-eyed, open mouthed horror.

And in the wake of this energy passed through the two of them, the screams beneath her taper into long and breathless wails, which form into a whining, whispering call for a mercy that cannot be given, as her entire body begins to freeze *solid,* becoming immobile as lake ice in January, until the ivory skin frosts the color of death in arctic winter, and snowy crystals begin to decorate even the black underwear fabric she is in.

In the aftermath of this trauma come and gone. At the beginning of a lifetime of sorrow. The ice goddess stands up tall and strong in the cold autumn rain. Feeling nothing of autumn's bitter warning from the clouds, nor the biting of its pre winter cold upon her skin.

Jonathan Lovejoy

Moonlight in Winter

"*The world is in shock this morning from reports out of Richland Hills, Virginia, of three cheerleaders from Amber West High School that were found dead in the last several days, two over the weekend. What has so many talking is not that all three girls were cheerleaders, but rather the details surrounding the bizarre nature of their deaths. One girl was discovered drowned in the swimming pool at the Sarah E. Josephine Recreation Center on campus, while the other two were found at home in their beds. But what has captured the imagination of people around the world is that*

two of the cheerleaders, eighteen year old Rosalyn Reynolds, and seventeen year old local beauty pageant queen Kelly LeMonde were found frozen completely solid in their beds this weekend. When the body of seventeen year old gymnastics champion Jennifer Lynn Johnson was found in the swimming pool, firemen had to chop through what was described as a layer of crystal clear ice, at least six inches thick covering the surface of the water. Adding to this strange mystery is the sudden disappearance of a fourth girl, seventeen year old Samantha Daley, who was the head varsity cheerleader at Amber West High School. Cora Leeds, the Associated Press."

How long did I really think it was going to last? This pathetic little attempt to catch a tiger by the tail? Internet news video, showing police tape around the recreation center, and across the lawn of one of those rich girls' houses, along with the NPR chatter boxes, all of it serves to flood my entire body with a dread I haven't felt since I came home that winter when she was thirteen years old, and saw her smoothing the face of a snow girl in the back yard with her bare hands. The so-called job I am trapped in has been called for the day, where my right to be 'sick' every once in a while finally kicks in, so I can stay at home and deal with this apocalyptic monster I have created.

As I wait for my daughter to come home, thoughts of my own mother haunt my desire to run like a scared rabbit to her uncaring arms, somewhere among the back roads near these Virginia woods, to tell her of what petals have grown from the flowers she planted a generation ago. But somehow, I know that Lucy Auburn can have no part of this Armageddon sway, and I am hopelessly alone, with no comfort from where it is that my beloved mother could have gone.

As the hours pass late into the morning, I know that aside from those dead girls' mothers, even moreso than the police themselves, I am more burdened by this than anyone else in the world, and for my sanity, I have to admit that as much as I have ever been, I now look toward every approaching hour with *fear.*

As if called forth by this revelation, by what cataclysm the third part of the truth hath done, the front door of my devastation opens, and in walks danger incarnate, in wet blonde hair and eyes burning the color of an arctic sky in winter.

I stand up from my hopeless trip through another Lifetime fantasy, stepping across the small livingroom with my hand raising up every step of the way, moving through her disbelieving stare to this inevitable conclusion, to bring my hand down across her face like thunder, which causes a shriek of shock and terror in the room.

"What the Hell gives you the right," I say, "to turn yourself into a murdering little *freak!"*

Touching her own face gently, where the red spot marks the burning on her skin, she stands up straight again, letting the sorrow and disappointment color her expression.

"It took you long enough didn't it?"

"Long enough to *what?"*

"To call me… a little freak."

And though I can see the effort, the effort to hold her teenage dignity, she blinks upon this last syllable spoken, to stab me in the heart, by way of a single teardrop on her cheek.

"I didn't mean it like that, Miranda, I swear to *God* I didn't."

"How did you mean it, Mom?"

"I meant that you *killed* three people. You murdered those girls with this thing you can do."

"And just what is this… *thing* I can do? Do you know? Are you smart enough to even begin to explain it?"

"The smartest people in the world couldn't explain this. It doesn't change the fact that you took it upon yourself to murder three innocent girls because they were cruel to one of your friends!"

"Innocent," she says, the pain in her face medicated by an inner smile. "Innocent. And what if I told you they were about as innocent as Ted Bundy?"

"What is that supposed to mean? What, did they beat her up or something?"

"I could take you for a drive if I wanted. If I thought that it mattered anymore. And I could show you something that would solve your little problem, of whether or not those dead bitches are innocent of anything."

"Innocent of… Miranda I still don't— "

"They *raped* her," she says. Staring me in the eyes. "They tied her to a wooden pole with a chain around her neck and handcuffs on her wrists. And they burned her while she was still alive."

"What?"

"You heard me! But you're just like everyone else would be if they found out. You don't believe it. Four sweet little cheerleaders, could never hurt a fly. Four sweet little cheerleaders. Why did they have to die?"

"Four? You mean there was another one? It was that head cheerleader they mentioned, wasn't it? Her name was... it was..."

"Samantha."

"Oh, dear Lord... no... did you—"

"You better believe it," she says. Sniffing, wiping her eyes. Walking calmly past me toward the stairs.

"You mean they... if they really did that then why couldn't you just go to the police? Then you could confess to what you've done."

"Are you serious?" she says. Stopping at the foot of the stairs. Burning an icy, bewildered stare.

"Miranda, you have no right to *kill!*"

"And what rights did Emily have, Mom? Didn't she have the right to live?"

"If you want to know the truth I don't give a *damn* about Emily Watson!"

And these words have their desired effect. To bathe my daughter's expression again with pain and suffering.

"If you don't care about Emily, then how can you care about me?"

"You *listen* to me," I say sharply, grabbing both her wrists hard. "I love you so much, sometimes I can't *breathe* when you're not around me. But what kind of a *sick* mother would I be if I let you go around killing people?"

"Do you have any idea what it's like," she says, staring at me as though racked with pity. Suddenly, I feel a cold strike the palms of both my hands, hard enough to make me pull away from her wrists like I had just grabbed two electric rods of ice cold steel.

"Do you have any idea," she says. "What it's like to be me? Do you want to trade places? Do you want to be able to do this?"

Memories of two wrists like pure ice are already burned into the palms of my hands, when she returns the favor and grabs *my* wrists, holding them in a grip too strong for any human to break, until my wrists feel as though the cold of a thousand winters is concentrated into them down to the bone. But she holds them there, listening to my words lose their cohesion, doubling me over with two maniacal screams of pure agony and terror.

She lets my wrists go in the nick of time, by the magic of what instincts she possesses, as I stand on the floor, a step below her towering high on the bottom step of the staircase. I cannot speak, but can only hold my wrists as though they have been burned.

"Do you want to trade places with that?" she says. "There is an *explosion* of cold inside me, Mom. You have no idea, the things I am capable of. The things that I can do. If I wanted, I could go down inside a volcano, and snuff it out like a candle. The world, Mom, is an evil, condemned place. There is a cold wind coming. And when the world gets wind of what I am capable of… there is going to be an apocalyptic *shock.*"

And to my horror, the girl who is my daughter stares down at me, through eyes the color of moonlight in winter. She turns to take the queen's ascension up the staircase, stepping in the throes of this regal crown, not bothering to grace me with more than a slight turn of her head.

"You may not give a damn about Emily. But I do."

Ice

Upon this, she ascends the steps to the upstairs hall, turning to stroll somewhere beyond my sight towards the queen's chambers. Toward the sanctuary of her upper room.

Jonathan Lovejoy

Christ the Redeemer

Jonathan Lovejoy

It's just enough to see a shooting star
To know you're never really far
It's just enough to see a shooting star
To know you're never really gone

Oh, please don't go
Let me have you just one moment more
Oh, all I need
All I want is just one moment more—

Mindy Smith

$\mathcal{W}$aterfalls around the world are the first to acknowledge the third part of the truth, giving in to what forces must bring about, when the air around them is reduced to apocalyptic, crystalline cold. Rivers have slowed from a trickle to a crawl, where the ice flows above them were once seen moving, to where now the tops have ceased their motion, to end all speculation about the future of running water in the open air. From beneath the surface of this freezing, from the top of the whispering of Angel Falls, to the bottom of the roaring monster at Niagara, the remaining water trickles free over the ice that has formed on the way down, to create a descending curtain of ice overnight, so that nature hath provided a still picture of the raging white waters that have come and gone.

From the warmest temperatures in 27 degree waiting in the still air at the tropics, to those that plunge to 88 degrees *below* through to the northern Tundra, winds of eschatology rise and blow with purpose beyond warning, to freeze every remaining drop of rain into a coating of ice along the surface, and eventually transform these hopeless droplets into deadly flakes of snow. Freezing rainstorms of hurricane force have blown their way ashore, having already covered the coastal cities and towns with the thickest sheets of ice known to man, where road signs along the highways are buried in thick, crystalline barriers to understanding, and many an overpass is crusted to the top of every passing truck as a cave of ice growing down, until the mouths of these ice caves are sealed, and impassable in the cold. Mountainous cicles of ice hang down from the interstate signs in deadly crystalline dagger, having fallen upon more than a passing car or two, with deathly consequences for the world weary travelers inside.

And when the salt trucks spread their melting false hope along the black topped lies of refuge and escape, the icy temperatures in the air rise just enough, so that the snows give way to freezing rains again, until the highways are coated in ice too thick to dream of melting, and every brave and wayward traveler creeps along in rolling caution in the wind. Poverty mothers from the mountains to the desert neighborhoods pour hot water in grieving over the windshields every morning, in desperation to see their way clear to roll over the icy streets to the factories, stores and offices where the dollar for survival is made.

And slowly, as the icy air moves and oppresses the Tropic of Cancer to the Tropic of Capricorn, the wind chills the hope that remains down to where the thermostats are 27 degrees below zero, marking themselves as the warmest places on the face of the earth. Further and further south from the Northern seas, icebergs drift with nary a hint toward melting, some of them drifting ashore nearby the great ocean cities, to add their jagged, snow white statement to the new landscape of humanity. In shipping lanes throughout the seven seas, ships from the equator to the arctic and Antarctic circles have discovered northern truth in southern waters, and southern, Antarctic truth in their Northern, tropical waters, as sheets of ice begin to appear many miles across, until ships are bound by the borders of a surface they cannot sail, as tropical waters have begun to look like those at the poles in winter. Visions of the earth from high above reveal a world of white decorated by smaller and smaller patches of blue, as every mile and inch of the seven seas begins to tell the tale, of an atmosphere burdened by the deepest cold in human history.

From along the Pacific Rim, to the blue lava eruptions of Indonesia, these lights have begun to cease their glow, as the quaking and rumbling of the earth produces no eruption to survive the melting walls of ice that pour in upon them, until what heat the earth may provide is buried deep within itself, beneath a surface bound and determined to stay buried in unfathomable, unquenchable, crystalline cold. From the mountain landscapes to the prairie plains where winds are adrift, forests are coated in layers of clear and frosted crystal, every leaf, every needle pine, every branch of every tree hung heavy with layers of ice and icicles hanging down, until standing beneath the tallest trees is a dire, and deadly proposition. Even from the heights of the great sequoias to the ground underneath at their feet, there extends some of the greatest woodland icicles in the world, grown like columns up from the icy ground itself, supported by the strength of branches that would not give in to the ice storms, until these columns of ice were touched all the way to the ground twenty stories below, where they gathered themselves an unmoveable anchor in the earth itself; towers of woodland ice as thick as trees, climbing 25 stories into the air overhead, known as the Sequoia Ice Forest, where the Pacific ice columns testify to the beginning of sorrows.

And these anomalies have not escaped the curiosities of manmade space in time, the arch of St. Louis per example, being supported now in every inch of its inner space with a permanent sheet of crystalline ice from the sky to the ground, where the rising and the setting sun shimmer boldly through. Along the bridge of the Golden Gate, every red inch is a prisoner of the crystalline glow in the rising and setting sun, with many columns of ice decorating the support cables from the high iron towers, to the parts that swing just above the streets below. The passengers roll across the streets of this red iron ice giant, this marvel of the modern world, gazing across the frozen waters of San Francisco Bay, that stretches into the distance like an arctic landscape to the horizon in either side of their journey.

From the frozen shores of the Pacific Ocean, across the ice covered Gulf of Mexico, over the icy landscape of the Tijuca Forest, down to where Christ the Redeemer towers above a humanity beyond Redemption, both of the outstretched arms sit atop of ice sheets all the way to the ground below, to remind the world of the Second Coming of power and glory, in the future beyond the ice and snow. This, as churches and cathedrals around the world are crushed and caved in by the heavy ice and snow storms, having taken tens of thousands in hopeless worship to a God they never really believed in before the ice came, while nearly half the earth's seven billion population is frozen to death, and buried in the cold.

Ice

From the crystal coated towers that stretch to the heavens in the far cities, to the icicle covered swings and climbing towers in the empty schoolyards and playgrounds, the children look to the men and women for answers to their naïve question, to fulfill the prophecy that foretells of wisdom brought forth from the mouths of babes, *Mommy, why is God so angry with the world?*

Why the cold?

I ponder this benign question. This casual observance, as I stroll the frozen Atlantic shores south, along the icy beaches of Cape Hatteras, marveling at the black and white striped simplicity that is the Cape Hatteras Lighthouse, and the upside down crystal spires that decorate it from the top halfway to the bottom.

Reports of what happened to the Statue of Liberty and the Freedom Tower would have been dismissed as mass delusion, if not for the fact that they both lie in ruins over the icy ground up north, the statue crushed to oblivion in a field of broken ice, and the fallen tower in a line of rubble stretched a half mile in one direction across the city floor. Residents all over the city claimed to have seen something in the shape of a hand in 50 stories of impossibility form in the midst of the storm, slamming itself into the tower with such force that the impact was heard across the entire city as the noise of an earthquake, which knocked the building off its foundation like a giant tree struck by lightning, causing it to fall nearly intact all the way down to the city floor below, dying in a thunderous cloud of rumbling, earth shaking devastation and debris, sending seven thousand unlucky souls to their icy graves in the storm. As to whether or not the piles of ice boulders scattered in the rubble are the remains of the icy hand of Judgment formed, who's to say?

My mind is ablaze with the weather witch my daughter became, the apocalyptic ice queen, whom I often saw in the open area of Bolden Park, in the early days of the ice storms, her arms stretched to the heavens, her eyes glowing the color of moonlight in winter.

Emily! Young woman of straw! My daughter gave her heart in hope and love to thee! I did not know you, my daughter's dearest Emily, only that thine was a soul of grief and mourning—a heart of dark destiny revealed. Oh, what tragic life thou hast lived and died, sister Emily, sister of pain, daughter of Fate! How could you have known, dear Emily, that you would be the catalyst to my daughter's apocalyptic heart, to fill her with the power of unearthly rage and vengeance, to multiply her sorrow as the stars of the Heavens, to send her ability into the skies over our horizon, to take away mankind's hope for the future, to deliver an apocalyptic warning to flee, to flee the divine wrath to come! My poor Emily, rest well in thy daily walk in Paradise, nearby the streets of that golden city, somewhere along the shores of Heaven.

As I look out over the frozen ice field that was once the Atlantic Ocean, I ponder this benign question, this casual observance, that still haunts me in my dreams.

Why the cold?

ABOUT THE AUTHOR

Jonathan Lovejoy is a graduate of the University of North Carolina at Greensboro, with a B.A. in Religious Studies, and a graduate of Liberty University with an M.A. in Theological Studies. He currently lives in Winston Salem, North Carolina.

For more info on the author's life and career, visit jonathanlovejoy.com

www.ingramcontent.com/pod-product-compliance
Lightning Source LLC
Chambersburg PA
CBHW061317170626
46817CB00001B/211